I0670663

HOLLOW TONGUE

RAW DOG
SCREAMING
PRESS

Published by Raw Dog Screaming Press
Bowie, MD

First Edition

Cover art copyright 2024 by Lynne Hansen
LynneHansenArt.com

Printed in the United States of America

ISBN: 978-1-947879-69-0
Library of Congress Control Number: 2024932727

RawDogScreaming.com

HOLLOW TONGUE

Eden Royce

Also by Eden Royce

Adult:

Who Lost, I Found: Stories

Children:

Root Magic

Conjure Island

Acknowledgments

I'm so grateful to have another book out in the world. The process for each one is always different, but no matter what else happens, I'm grateful to speak on the page once again.

Thank you to my family both here and gone. You have influenced me in some beautiful, tender, fierce, and unforgettable ways. I think of you often.

Thanks, Mom, for everything.

Thank you to my husband, for reading an early draft of this book, encouraging me to send it in, and for just being wonderful.

To Tony for giving such excellent feedback, and making great coffee recommendations.

To R.J. Joseph and the entire team at Raw Dog Screaming Press for selecting this story to be a part of their new horror novella series. I'm honored. Enormous thanks to Lynne Hansen for creating a beautiful, eerie cover.

As always, boundless thanks to my readers for your support and to the reviewers who give the most thoughtful commentary on my work. I see you and I appreciate you.

The Horror welcomes her, again,

—Emily Dickenson

On Memory

Somewhere in my reading, I came across a quote: "It is only with the greatest care that memory can be kept from becoming a prison or a gallows." My personal belief, however, is that memory is more akin to a chain, forged link by iron link, that tethers us to our experiences. There are things to which we are glad to be tethered—memories of joy, love, triumph—but there are other, darker things as well—terror, trauma, sorrow—that cling to our souls like the webs of a great spider. And while these links may be invisible, the things to which they bind us are often physical: a person, a scent, a taste…a house. So it is in this entry of the Selected Papers from the Consortium for the Study of Anomalous Phenomena, or SPECSAP, as I've taken to shortening it in my references.

In Eden Royce's *Hollow Tongue*, memory is how we relate to the protagonist—seeing the trauma that led her to where she is today, and how it drags her back to the place it all began. Memory takes many forms in this story: tether, prison, flog, and, for lack of a better word, a mutagen.

I'm unsure of who the self-proclaimed "Weaver" —the penperson for the previous introduction—is, however, their point on memory as fickle and flighty, yet vicious, was spot on. In the case of *Hollow Tongue*, it affects how the protagonist interacts with the world and how she perceives herself. From her emotional responses to her smell, Maxine is constantly at war with the memories of the trauma inflicted on her by her father—and in some ways, her mother as well. Home, to her, is the dwelling place of a monster, and the shadow of that thing looms over her.

One of these papers, *12 Hours*, centralizes our thoughts on the present—the now—through the eyes of the taxi driver as he experiences everything around him, with no memory of how he ended up in his situation. *Asylum* expanded this, tying the present experiences of its characters back to their trauma and how it bound them into a reasonable facsimile of a family. *Hollow Tongue* is a story that lives in the broken past of Maxine's life and the isolation of her present. It unfolds in glimpses of memory, recollections that rise unbidden to the surface.

Trauma does not always bind people together. Sometimes it separates. Sometimes it changes—for better, or for worse. I'll leave you to contemplate Maxine's metamorphosis yourself, how her trauma cocooned her and brought out something new.

But know this: she isn't the only thing that's changed since she left home.

It feels strange to wish you enjoyment in your trip down Maxine's fraught and tumultuous memory lane, but it won't stop me from doing so. This is a truly special document that we are privileged to share with you, one of a woman haunted by a past that burrows into her soul and hopes to suck her dry with its hollow tongue.

From the Desk of [Redacted],
Librarian of the Consortium for the Study of Anomalous Phenomena

ONE

They would eat us, if they could.

The man in the video Maxine is watching is small, fragile-looking, with large, wide eyes. Intense enough that her mama would have called them crazy eyes. When she was younger, she used to tell her mama not to use that word, but Mama would suck her teeth and say, "Nothin' wrong with being crazy. Crazy might save you one day."

Maxine sucks her teeth, too, remembering, while the hot crab dip she took out of the oven cools to an edible temperature on the table in her eat-in kitchen. She's treated herself to the crab meat, just enough to make a dip, not a full lump crabcake, and the fragrant dish sits waiting, while she goes to pour herself a drink. It takes longer now, to cross the kitchen with her injured leg, but she manages it this time without grunting. Jaw set, she fills a glass with iced tea.

The man in the video says the phrase in all seriousness. Briefly, she wonders if the scientist Mama used to work for looks the same. Then he smiles as an afterthought, as though someone told him in the past to soften his intensity for the comfort of others. His smile is anything but comforting, though. It's a rictus, a frozen show of bone and pink flesh that makes him look more like a grotesque puppet than the scientist the lower third says he is. In that smile, he acknowledges what he says is beyond the pale. No one wants to know that something so small and beautiful desires us for its food.

Why does the algorithm recommend this foolishness? She's never watched a video on insects before, why would she want to now? Maxine closes it, puts on her favorite oldies playlist instead. Disco, the sound she and her mother used to clean the house to, oozes through the speakers of her phone. When she returns to the table, a butterfly, purple and black and blue and yellow—what bruise colors looked like on her light brown skin—has perched in the middle of her casserole dish. The sliding door onto the balcony of her apartment is open to late afternoon, the warm from the oven dish enough to lure the creature in to feed.

It perches prettily on the crisp-topped crab spread like a living garnish, its bruised-flesh wings batting in delight as it sucks up the moisture from the last meal she will ever buy with her salary from the packaging company. They've laid her off after seven months, and while it may have had to do with her inability to crouch and bend the way she used to, surely there was something she could have done to stay employed.

But the pro-bono attorney she'd spoken to doesn't think so. A condition of her employment was being able to lift 30 pounds and she could no longer fulfill that requirement. *Be thankful for such a generous severance package*, he'd said as he gathered his paperwork, in a hurry to get to his next chance to deliver bad news.

By the time she'd managed to push back from her table, and lever herself to a standing position, he was at the door turning the knob. It didn't move and she made her way across the living room with pain-filled glee, watching his distress at seeing her unbalanced movements. He pulled on the deadbolt lock and key again in an effort to leave.

Her pleasure then turned to irritation. He couldn't wait to get out of her home. It was a small apartment, all she could afford in D.C., where the rents were high and the possibility of her saving enough for a down payment for a home was the equivalent of finding a unicorn to lie in her lap. She bit her lip against the ache. And it was just a limp, for God's sake. Honestly, it was more of a stiff-legged shuffle, rock to the side, lift and thrust to her gait. Maxine let out a dark chuckle. Described like that, her walk sounded like the steps to a line dance. Tariq might have still loved her then, as he loved any dance he had to spend time mastering. Not so much with women.

She'd met the attorney at the door and ignored his shrinking back to give her room. "There's a trick to getting it open." She'd twisted the key in the lock and the doorknob at the same time, in different directions and with a squeak the door swung open. Crisp air flooded the house, sending a chill through her. The attorney had been halfway down the stairs before he'd thrown back over his shoulder that she could call him if anything else came up.

Yeah, right.

She comes back to the present in a rush, like the jolt when someone slams on the brakes, the seatbelt yanking your body back from certain mutilation. For a moment, she watches the intruder. This food thief, she is stunned at its audacity. She considers filming the phenomenon, but quick movements are alien to her now. Instead, she tries to shoo it away with the mail she'd retrieved earlier, but the butterfly is reluctant to leave its prize. Only when she tries to pick it up in cupped palms does it finally, drunkenly depart the way it had come.

Maxine pats the sweat from her brow. Having to rush over to remove the intruder, even that small movement irritates her leg. She smoothes the wayward puff of her hair back from her face with one hand and leans against the counter to catch her breath. She fans herself with the mail, ready to toss once she's cooler, until her own name printed on one envelope catches her eye. Junk mail, flyers, and solicitations to the "Current Occupant" are the only physical mail she receives. More confused than concerned, she plucks a paring knife out of the block near the stove and plops her weight down in a chair. The return address is printed on an inexpensive white business-sized envelope in blue ink:

TruNational Bank
P.O. Box 124486
Charleston, SC 29403

A missive from home, then.

Although she's been away for years, Maxine considers The Chuck to be home. No matter how much it had hurt her, or how long she spent living in D.C., Chucktown has wormed its way into her core. Mama or Daddy sending a letter is a thin hope anyway; they believe it's her duty to check on them. She's their only child, eternally a child in their eyes even though she is twenty-five. Maxine has only reached out a few times in those years; no reason for a change now.

She slips the knife between the folds of the envelope and rends it open, leaving a trail of whitened dust on the air. She reads the contents, one sheet of standard paper laser printed with the bank's letterhead and signed by the branch manager, whose name she doesn't recognize. Informing her that if payment for the safe deposit box listed with her and her mother's names was not received within ten days of the letter's date, the box would be drilled open, the contents emptied, logged, then turned over to the state as abandoned property. So, seven years have passed since she left. If this letter has found her, Maxine knows that means Mama got out.

After returning the letter to the envelope, she takes slow, even breaths to calm her speeding heart. The scent of the crab spread clouds the room. She ignores it, and the pain in her leg when she rocks the stool back on its legs and gets up, hobbling around her efficiency kitchen. Maxine wants to laugh, but she is too stunned to be thrilled. She wonders how Daddy is taking Mama's absence and if he is sorry yet. A prickle of hurt needles through her heart.

Why hasn't Mama tried to call or email? Had she just run for the hills and everyone else be damned? Maxine's read somewhere once that trauma makes you cruel. Or is it terror? Both apply, and to both her and Mama. She can't begrudge her mother anything she decides to do to celebrate her freedom. Maxine's been able to leave because Mama had made a way for her to; there is no telling what Daddy had done when she wasn't there to share in the duty of dispelling his anger. She should be glad Mama's finally out of that house.

Mama's out. Mama's out. She does her rocking, walking dance to the beat of those words. *Mama's out. Mama's out.* Either that or she's dead. No matter what, Maxine now had to go home to see which was true. And to clear out the contents of that safe deposit box.

If Max is honest with herself, she doesn't remember what's in the box, but she remembers her promise to clean it out if anything happens to her mother. Impossible to let anything of her family's go to the state. Maybe Mama had emptied the safe deposit box before she left, and just forgot to close it out with the bank before heading…where?

The timing of the letter is uncanny, and it fits perfectly in the image she has of returning home to tell Daddy how he can't hurt Mama or her anymore, ever. With her fork, she digs into the middle of the crab, where the thief had perched and eats a mouthful of the still-warm spread. Crackers be damned, it's good. She covers the tray with foil to save for later as she has more pressing work to do. She's not desperate yet, but she has no plans to be before she can secure herself a chance to regroup. This meal is courtesy of the last of her severance and soon she'll have to find a job that can accommodate her injury or start using her savings or cash in her 401(k).

No choice now. She puts the letter in her bag. Ten days from the date of the letter. So, eight days to fix this. This situation solves a lot of problems, one of them with her dad. She rips the letter she has started writing to him from the notebook and touches it to the lemon and bay candle flickering on the countertop.

Dad,

I know it's been a while but I need to come home. It's a long story and it'll only be for a little while. I just

Maxine still isn't able to think of words that would convince her father to allow her back in the house without angering him to the point he takes it out on her mother. Now, there's no need. The man who had made life hell for her growing up is still her father and she doesn't need to explain herself ahead of her arrival. Plenty of time once she gets there. He's never going to kick her out, she's sure of that. Pretty sure. She holds the paper as it burns halfway, then she tosses the remains of the letter into a pan on the stove and goes to pack.

TWO

Something changed as Max got closer to home. Maybe it was all of the reminicing she'd done throughout the drive. She tried calling her father from the car, but he didn't pick up any of the four times she rang. Maybe he didn't recognize the number and refused to answer. Well, she refused to leave a message, so there they were. So much for breaking up the drive with some uncomfortable conversation. Eight hours of driving the black ribbon of road was painful. Not simply because of her damaged leg's immobility, but the rote monotony of that drive from DC to The Chuck—especially those last three hours—that obliged her to think of the past she was approaching. The road seemed to be taking her downhill to a place she had escaped from years ago.

I'm just trying to look out for you.

Well, don't!

Baby, we just want you to have a good man. Somebody to care for you.

I don't want a man.

A pause. *You want a woman?*

I don't want anything, anyone. Just leave me alone!

The rules, the rituals, the standards she had to hit each and every time. There was no space for failure, no breaks from the tedium.

Expectation choked her. Daddy's record played on repeat for years until one day, Max'd left for good.

Had she been too impulsive in leaving without taking Mama with her? Max bit at her lip as she glanced in her mirrors and changed lanes. She'd only just turned eighteen herself when Mama had pushed her to leave. Should she have insisted on staying until they could both get away? Max was their only child, what the folks called *ol' people churn*. Children born to parents later in life. Her mother had been forty-two when she was born and her father had been forty-five. And they had a way of bringing up children that was from a generation before hers.

Marry, then have children. At least one of them would be someone to take care of you when you can't do for yourself. Even if you can't marry, at least provide the children...

Well, she can't do that. Not anymore.

Max drains the rest of her coffee as she takes the exit off I-26 toward the house. Already, she can smell the scent of the city through her open window: the heat, the sea, the sweet funk of the pluff mud of the marshes. She's tapping her non-driving foot and she has to remind herself that she can handle Daddy now. She's not a baby any longer, and his words don't matter.

Not anymore.

It was a monstrosity.

The house on Sans Souci Street where she'd grown up had changed. Chipped brick, exposed sun-bleached wood, paint peeling in places. Darkened in other places by a moss/mold hybrid that clung to wood and brick alike. Grass on either side of it a frayed yellow ochre. A husk, an abandoned cocoon that had one held a prosperous, growing family. Still, the yellowed grass had been cut, the sparse hedges trimmed.

She pushed the car door open, swung her left leg out, then eased her right one around, lifting it a bit with her right hand to clear the lip of the car's low footwell. It had supposedly healed all it was going to, according to the doctor. Her physical therapist said the stiffness would return whenever she stayed immobile for too long. The eight-hour drive—and the years away from home—were long enough to stay immobile. Her relationship with her mother had made no progress in all that time.

Maxine groaned at the movement of her leg; when she put her weight on it, it buckled for a moment, causing her to lean heavily against the roof of the car. *Breathe. Breathe through it, direct it out.* The refrain from her PT echoed. It had become a habit now. Maybe if she'd learned to breathe through pain all those years ago…

But she hadn't. And now she was back.

Hand go, hand come.

Mama had always said that. A refrain she'd learned from the old people in the neighborhood over the years. They were all gone now. Their house was one of the only ones not taken over by gentrification, but it was also the only one in such a state. Backyard choked with bushes and vines, in desperate need of paint. Some windows still had boards of plywood nailed over them from the last hurricane. Did it leak, she wondered? Fine time to ask now, when she didn't have anywhere else to go.

"You Genevieve gal?"

The call came from behind her and as Maxine wasn't expecting anyone around here to remember her, she jumped. Spun to face the speaker, twisting her leg in the process. Cursed. Through gritted teeth, she addressed the old man who'd called to her.

"That's me." She grunted softly, pressing the heel of her hand just below her hip. It didn't help with the pain, but it made her feel more steady. Her physical therapist might have been right about it being too early to stop using the cane. But her pride had made her pack it in the trunk instead of carrying it with her in the car. The passenger seat was reserved for her pocketbook, a bag of white grapes, and a few individual bags of salt and vinegar potato chips.

"Thought so." His dark brown face was the way old Black people in the South aged. Not wrinkling, but a softening of the skin, a settling into surrender instead of resistance as part of life. The way a face looks when you've set your own burdens down or turned them over to the next generation.

"You visitin'?"

He had a lawnmower with him, and held a big, plastic garbage can of tools in one ungloved hand. Probably this was the man who had done the gardening. The front yard *was* neat and tidy. Mama would have given him a few dollars, but Maxine did not. If he liked to keep other people's yards clean, that must be enough for him.

"Not this time. Moving in." She shuffled her weight to her good leg. "Did you do the yard work out here?"

"Yep. I was out doing mine, and I figured... why not? Used to have a lotta business but ain't nuttin but white folks round here now. Pretty much at my limit anyways."

"So, I won't be able to ask if you'll do the back yard too?"

His eyes widened, showing the white around dark brown eyes rimmed with the blue of age. "Not that yard, not no time soon." Then he seemed to gather himself with a shrug that said, *These churn got nerve.* "Sides, I'm moving. Got me a nice little condo cross the river."

Many thought Black neighborhoods were declining in this area because of gentrification. While that was true, another part of it was due to the local Black population abandoning the community mindset that had once organized sit-ins and boycotts and rallies. Now that things were marginally better for a few, everyone wanted to move out of the historically Black areas for better opportunities, better schools, better chances. But not Daddy. He was here for the long haul. Come what may.

Not that Max could talk. She'd left as soon as she was able. Eighteen with a diploma in one hand and Mama's savings in the other. She'd left at Mama's pleading. *If I stay, he'll let you go.* She'd whispered. For once in her life, Max had listened. She took the money, bought a bus ticket, and hauled ass.

"Figures. I'll find someone."

The gardener man had no recommendations. "How ya Mama?"

Maxine had no idea.

Part of her wanted to say she was fine, just to be done with the conversation. Saying, *You'd know better than I would.* That occurred to her as well. But that wouldn't get her anywhere and airing her family's laundry wasn't something she was raised to do. That realization made the decision for her. She'd been gone from this place for long enough to do what she thought was right, to shrug off the lessons of her youth.

"She left Daddy, so I don't know."

"Oh, I see," he said, with a look of confusion on his face.

Whether that confusion was because her mother had left her father or because their only daughter was bold enough to tell their business, she didn't know or care. She did note that the man didn't ask how her father was doing.

No one ever knew exactly what went on behind closed doors in a household, but Daddy had been public enough with his words and actions that their neighbors had always given the entire family a wide berth. There'd been no calling the police during any of their arguments, though. That would have brought a whole other level of problem. So, the Forest family's problems festered within the walls of the house.

"But, I'm sure she's good wherever she is."

She shaded her eyes from the glaring, relentless sun with a cupped palm. The February weather hadn't fully warmed up yet. Chill still lay in the air. But the reflection of the sun on the windows was piercing. If she was tired of questions, she wouldn't want to hire this man to do the gardening. He was the type to poke and prod and bring up stories and people she'd rather forget. She'd be better off doing it herself. At least then she could tell the PT she was getting some exercise.

"I'm Maxine, by the way. Max."

He looked her up and down, lips tight. Then he held his chin up high. "Mister Green," he offered, emphasizing the title. He didn't offer his first name and she didn't ask. It wasn't the done thing and it would immediately mark her as having changed. Left the old ways behind.

She nodded. "Well, Mister Green. I just got off the road, so I'm ready to lay this body down for a bit."

He nodded. "Good luck to you, Maxine."

"Oh, Max is fine." Was it? She always told people in D.C. to call her by her full name.

He waved a hand at her as he turned away, pulling the lawnmower and the garbage can behind him. Mister Green might have thought he was muttering to himself as he left, but she heard him perfectly well.

"I don't know why you young ladies don't do something with your hair no more. Nothing worse than a yellow gal with a picky head."

Max sank her fingers into her Afro and tugged the coils into place where the headrest of the car had flattened them. It was nothing she hadn't heard before. But for some reason, the comment slipped under the surface of her skin. She separated her coils and tugged harder for a moment, like pulling a bee stinger out before it worked its way deeper.

She chuckled, a short dry cough of a laugh, then turned away from the old man's retreating form. She rang the doorbell. No answer. Not really surprising because Daddy rarely wanted to answer the door. That had been her job growing up. No matter what she was doing, she had to stop and see who was visiting. It was because she was the youngest, Mama would say as she snapped beans at the dining room table, the TV blaring out an advertisement during her stories. *You have the most energy, and it'll only take you a moment.*

Both her parents had sent her off on errands like that as girl. Run and get me a drink. Run and answer the door. Run and run and run. No matter what she might have been doing. Schoolwork, talking on the phone. No matter. Run.

Mister Green had said he hadn't seen Daddy in a while and if he wasn't out after dark, that was probably true. She'd prepared herself for finding Daddy drunk inside. If he was going to be nasty she could handle it now. He'd never put his hands on either one of them, her or Mama. So he'd been shocked when she'd said he was abusive. *I never raised my hand to you, Max. Never.*

No, he hadn't, she admitted. But, still…

She squared her shoulders and rang again. Knocked briskly on the window until she was concerned it would fall out. Had he passed out inside, sick from drink? Jeez-us, that was the last thing she needed: having to dry him out while she wanted to tell him his words didn't matter to her anymore.

It was time to stop waiting for permission to enter and let herself into the house and lay her body down, only briefly wondering why she'd used the phrase old people used for death. Her old house key had gone dull with disuse, and the doorknob's faux brass was peeling off, but they both turned easily enough. Without a creak, the door opened.

Chimes rang. A cacophony of sleigh bells Mama had put on the doorknob one Christmas and never taken off. Like a herald's trumpet, it announced her arrival into the darkened house. A wash of air, hot as breath, greeted her despite the chilled air outside.

As a girl, Maxine had thought the house on Sans Souci was grand, and she'd run along the polished hardwood floors in her socked feet, sliding until she reached the end of the hallway. Past Mama and Daddy's room and the room where Gramma had died, past the linen closet and the big mirror opposite the front door. The mirror was there to keep away evil spirits, just the sight of their own horrific nature would be enough to send them in flight for their life. Like so many things her parents had told her growing up, Maxine just took it for granted as being true. Not believing it wholeheartedly like a faithful devotee or anything, but she hadn't questioned it.

Now, the house could be full of anything. There were no more mirrors.

The years had gone by so fast. Over the years she'd moved six times. Six times in seven years was a lot for anyone. She'd been running. From something. What, she couldn't name. Maybe herself. But in the end, she'd run until she ran into her own reflection. And it had sent her scurrying home. She closed the door behind her and let the house welcome her back.

THREE

A house is the worst kind of monster. It is probably, more likely, a time-machine of the wickedest kind. With its inertia, its inaction, or rather, its action of constancy through the passing days, years, decades, it preserves itself. The same carpet, the same artwork, the same furniture, the same creaks and moans. Along with that preservation, it also maintains an image, a memory of us as we once were. So when we step through its doors, we are transported back through time, to a moment where we were perhaps at our most vulnerable.

If those moments or days or years or decades were warm, healthy, positive ones the memory is tender, heart-softening: a little bittersweet hint of nostalgia, a burnt, sweet caramel running over the history of our lives. If those moments were not warm and healthy, it becomes a horror that lives inside of us, fermenting like rotting fruit, seemingly perfectly fine on the outside, but at the slightest prodding bursts, releasing its decay.

The house transports you to a time in your life that you thought you'd forgotten about, but one your brain had bookmarked. And without your permission, it takes you back—body and mind—to that saved place. To that person you used to be. And it holds you there. Cocooned and soaking in the murky soup of memory. Old voices, old names, old pains attaching once again to the new us that we have so carefully crafted, working their way past the thin outer shell of who we are now to the soft meat of childhood where we were perhaps our most impressionable, our most vulnerable.

Maybe the real horror is how quickly, how easily, we remember.

FOUR

This was once the place she looked forward to, especially after a bone-chilling walk home from school in calf-deep flood waters. Max used to climb the front steps, open the door to this house and sigh at its warmth. After shedding her umbrella and raincoat in the bathtub, she would go into the kitchen, where Mama would have something delicious-smelling in the oven. Max would lean her back against the oven door, drawing its heat into her skin, reveling in being home.

Now the only scent here was the musty smell of a closed-up house. A fine layer of dust lay everywhere. While shadows hovered in the dim light, Max could tell the furniture was all the same, laid out in the same places so the indentations in the rugs would never come out. She shook her head as she flicked on the ceiling light. Illumination flickered to life, filling the path from the front door deeper into the center of the house. She needed to check to see if everything was in order, before she sat down.

"Daddy?" she called.

Silence replied, and she called again, louder, to no avail. She dragged her rolling suitcase behind her as she strode further inside, her sneakers making no sound.

Every framed picture was identical. The kitchen had the same avocado-hued fridge and oven. Across the room, a bar table and four long-legged chairs. Once the house had been filled with people, folks from the neighborhood and Mama and Daddy's friends. Card parties and piña coladas made in the ancient, even then, Oster blender. Trays of food and laughter and music and dancing.

All gone.

"Daddy, it's me! You here?"

It was possible he wasn't. He had no idea she was coming, not for her lack of trying. She checked her phone. It was only just after two in the afternoon, so he could be out anywhere: buying groceries, drinking at a bar, over at some friend's house. Since he'd had to stop driving because of his eyesight, it was impossible to tell when he was in and when he wasn't. She just had to check the house over to make sure he wasn't dead somewhere, then wait for him to return.

The house, at least, seemed happy to see her. It was a time capsule, a ghost to its own self, trapped in space and a shape that belonged to another age. With her uneven gait, Max strolled the hallways looking into the rooms, to see the same art, the same floor coverings, the same furniture, all in the exact spaces they had been when she left. The dining room was like stepping into a Polaroid picture. Even without the good dusting it clearly needed, there was still a gloss to this room. A shine of use and wear that would not diminish. She flicked on the light and the illumination of the chandelier glittered over the accumulated dust and particles. A metallic shimmer lay on the wooden table, the sideboard, and the china cabinet. All furniture she didn't have back in her old place.

Her apartment had one room for her to cook, eat, sleep, and live—that was the only place to commune with her memories. Her dishes, pots and pans lived in the opposite side of the same cabinets as her clothes. She didn't have table linens to store and her table wasn't real wood; it was a secondhand number she could wipe clean with a wet rag. Did she really miss this house? Was her life in D.C. better—not knowing if her parents were alive or dead? This house— the people in it—had hurt her, but had it been any worse than what mangled her leg? Was anywhere safe? She flicked off the overhead light, leaving only the sunlight through the sheer curtains to filter in.

Max left her suitcase in the hall; her leg stinging and burning deep in the joint of her hip and in the surrounding muscle of her butt and thigh. The movement made it hurt more, but she knew it was important to walk the stiffness out. She glanced up to make sure the curtains were closed, and pulled down her yoga pants.

Raised, twisted skin greeted her. Thick with keloid scaring, shiny as though stretched and oiled, edged with a rim of darker skin. It twisted like a river, running from below her hip to just above her knee. The one in the middle of her chest, was smaller, although no less twisted. She touched it gingerly, as she had a thousand times before, remembering lying on the floor of that bodega, the air full of the smell of cordite and her mouth full of the flavor of copper.

She'd been FaceTiming with Tariq, in an argument about who was coming over to whose house. At the counter, quick, raised voices, sounds of a scuffle, then searing heat thudding into her once, twice, three times. She staggered, the wall of chips falling backwards. Saw the red staining her pale peach jumpsuit. It would never come out. It was silk. She'd saved for it. Silk stained. She fell then, comically, into the wire rack, chips flying everywhere; a few bags popped open under her weight, sounding frightfully like more gunshot. She blinked up at the filthy ceiling, water-stained a rusty brown, and beginning to warp.

"Oh shit."

That was Tariq, but she couldn't talk to him. Words didn't come, only her breath. She closed her eyes, tried breathing slow and shallow. Hadn't that been how MLK survived that stabbing in jail? Yeah, it was, but when they'd shot him, he'd died.

Heavy footfalls entered the space some time later. They didn't check on her.

"Three dead. Two males, one female. Black."

The paramedics had shown up anyway.

"She's alive."

Curses accompanied their work and a mask descended on her face. She clutched the phone, knowing it was her only proof. Proof of life.

Max pulled up her pants, tucked away the memory. She should have checked the house first before getting settled. Suppose there was some door or window open? Her sense of safety since the accident and her subsequent hospital stay was warped. She didn't care as much about strangers seeing her naked but she checked her surroundings more often than was likely necessary. Groaning, she headed down the hall. It was time for a pain pill, but that would have to wait until she could get some food.

Dust lay on the kitchen surfaces, but there were no dirty dishes or old food around. She pulled open the fridge to find it empty and surprisingly clean—only beer and some condiments. Nothing she wanted in here. Dad's idea of a well-stocked fridge was beer, butter, and condiments. A fuzz-covered jar of some reddish paste went right in the trash, along with a greenish loaf of bread.

The cupboards held a half-empty bag of sugar, some boxes of quick grits, a full jar of honey, a few dented cans of flake tuna. Nothing fresh. She would have to go to the store. But today, she would order delivery; she didn't have energy for anything else. She'd call for a pizza, then tomorrow she'd shop for groceries, in preparation for the return of her father and his hangover.

She retrieved her bag from the hallway and returned to the kitchen, then took out handfuls of dirty laundry and stuffed them in the washer. The washing powder was stiff, dried into chunks, but with a firm thud on the counter, enough separated into fine grains to fill the washing tray. There was no fabric softener, so she just hoped the machine still worked or she would be left with another mess to straighten out. A relieved sigh escaped her when the washer started up, churned loudly for a few tense moments before finally settling into the familiar hum of the cotton cycle. Might as well have a look around, she had an hour to kill.

When she pushed the door to her parent's bedroom, it swung open soundlessly. Save for the crumpled bed clothes, this room was unchanged. Queen-sized bed, mirrored dresser, a print of some pastoral landscape of a place none of them had ever been framed on one wall, a reproduction of a bouquet of flowers framed on another. The flowers drifted in mid-air, not held by vase or hand or table. It hit her then, the smell. Or rather the absence of it. Not the fresh smell of recent cleaning or the rank of liquor sweat. Nothing. She checked the window and it wasn't open. She closed the door and headed for the guest room.

It was pristine in here. A room rarely used since her grandma had passed. A photograph, that's what this room was. Exactly as it had been when she'd left. The wall color, a dusty rose that matched the roses on the bedspread and the ones carved into the dresser and its mirror. Curtains tied back to let in a wedge of sunlight that served to highlight the dust motes Max had disturbed with her presence. She felt as though she'd smudged a newly cleaned car or muddied a freshly-mopped floor. Like she was somewhere she shouldn't be.

She moved an amber blown glass ashtray from the table in the hall. It was empty, but she recalled it being used, the cloud of tobacco smoke hovering in the dining room when Daddy's friends were over. He would call to her to greet them, these grown men. Calling them her uncles when she knew he didn't have any brothers. *Give your Uncle Folksy a hug now.* That ashtray filled almost to overflowing, and the table it sat on littered with Schlitz cans with the blue bull on them. And wanting to please him, she would hesitantly slink over, head averted and present herself for hugging. The men laughed, all taking their turns to hug her tight against their scratchy beards, saturated with smoke and Old Spice before Daddy would allow her to return to her room. Often, she would skulk away, and as quietly as she could, run hot water in the bathroom basin and wash off the scent of their cologne.

The complexities of it all. Did it matter now? Max had gotten out, and Mama had managed to leave Daddy somehow. But where was he? She'd assumed he was out on some bender, drinking away his memories, but what if Mama had … done something?

The only way she knew about Mama's departure was the letter that had arrived from the state's abandoned property department. She was listed on their records as co-owner and they had been unable to locate her mother. But somehow they'd found her in D.C. What had Mama left in that safe deposit box? Max rubbed her arms, feeling a chill that had nothing to do with the temperature outside. People pushed to their limits did horrible things, unthinkable things in order to get free of destructive situations. Was this one of those situations? She fisted her hand and beat it against her injured leg, the pain helping her focus. Why had she felt a streak of sympathy for her father? If Mama had done the worst, why? Why hadn't she come to Max for help before taking such a drastic step?

She wouldn't have. Not Mama. She would never have killed Daddy, no matter what. She wouldn't even call the police on him, so killing him herself was out of the question. But the overgrown back yard and Mr. Green's odd behavior had her wondering.

When would she consider him missing?

Daddy was nowhere to be found and she had no idea where to start looking. Should she even bother reporting it? How long had Mama been gone? If the police came here and started looking around, they might find some clue to implicate her mother and Max couldn't let that happen. Mama deserved some peace. She wasn't proud of it, but she took out her phone and looked up how long it would take to declare someone legally dead without a body. Five years in South Carolina. It was called presumption of death and she began memorizing section 62-5-07, rule five of the probate code.

A person whose death is not established under the preceding paragraphs who is absent for a continuous period of five years, during which he has not been heard from, and whose absence is not satisfactorily explained after diligent search or inquiry, is presumed to be dead.

The clock counter would start when she reported him missing, but it would be just like her father to turn up the moment she went to get any help. If Max was right, Mama wouldn't show herself, not now. Once dead, Max would be Daddy's only known next of kin and the beneficiary of his estate. Likely her mother didn't want anything of his, anyway.

The house was all he had, really. Blindfolded, she could still navigate this house if she needed to. It was that exact, the floor plan imprinted on her mind, pulling her once again down its hallways to each and every room. Each and every room a horror unto itself.

Even in this place of everyday horrors, Max could not imagine her mother killing her father. Mama had endured Daddy for so long, she had built up a way to get around him, his moods, his unrealistic thought processes that somehow always brought him to the conclusion that Mama's actions were disrespectful to him.

No, Max was back at her original idea of him being out drinking. Of course he was. It wasn't even noon, but some place was open and selling boilermakers.

FIVE

With reverence, she entered the living room. A place she had never been allowed, unless summoned to greet a friend of the family she didn't know or hadn't met outside of when she was a babe in arms. Still, she'd been expected to welcome visitors with open arms, physical affection, or be deemed an embarrassment. She walked into the room now, the ache in her leg for the moment forgotten. It was a holy place, a place where she'd made sacrifices of herself; her own body given up for someone she could never recall.

She submitted to the hugs and the cheek kisses, and the lap sitting, like she was some kind of ornamental doll. After a time, these guests would pat her on the head or shoulder, the signal that she had served her time in their presence and she was dismissed.

Decades later, she sat where they had, directly on the sofa, not on a lap or the arm of a chair. Deep breath in, she took a long look around the room at the three other chairs, the coffee table littered with old books and a candy jar of brightly-colored sweets that had long ago solidified together into one grotesque aberration of flavor and wondered why she had wanted entry to this room so badly.

The view was different from here. She ran her palm over the fabric cushion, the carved wood of the backrest. They hovered here, the memories of those guests. A shadow world of smiles and cigarette ash tapped into amber ashtrays, of nugget rings and splash cologne. Maxine stood. The garden would have some rosemary she could burn to get them out.

Otherwise, inside the house wasn't bad. It was clean enough for a person of her father's age—just as clean as her previous abode had been, to be honest. The house creaked when she moved through it, as if responding to her thoughts, and she shuddered. Maxine wasn't used to living in a place that spoke anymore. The places she'd lived were newer, if she could get them. Free of creaks and squeaks and sounds too much like the voices of family.

Noise. She needed that now. Why hadn't she brought a radio with her so she didn't have to drain her phone battery? Maxine sucked her teeth, then brought up a playlist on her phone. One she would have worked out to if she worked out. Upbeat, dancy, you-got-this-girl music accompanied her trip to the linen closet to change the sheets on the guest room bed. She wasn't ready to sleep in her old bedroom just yet.

She cracked a window to let the stale, tight smell out. A cool breeze flooded in, rustling the thick curtains. When she took her hand away from a fold in the curtain, a clingy film stuck to her skin. It was grayish white, like a cobweb, and she peeled it away with disgust and flushed it down the toilet.

Don't touch my dress! You're dirty, Max. Wash those filthy hands.

Mama. She'd been wearing her white usher's uniform about to go to church to some function. Max had been outside, doing God knew what, and wanted to hug her before she left. But Mama'd shuffled backwards, and held her gloved hands out as a warning.

Max strode over to the en suite bathroom in all its pink glory, turned the taps on full blast and shoved her hands under the running water. Rubbed them together to get the clinging stickiness off. After washing her hands thoroughly with the ancient soap, she slumped against the wall. She was tired of exploring, remembering. Her leg was burning and she wanted to eat, take her meds, and rest. Anything else could wait until after that. She dialed up Trattoria, her old favorite pizza place—they didn't have online ordering—and gave the guy who answered her order, being indulgent with her toppings.

The scent of gardenias blanketed her then, a ghostly visitor reminding her of Mama. She looked around, then laughed at herself. Mama wasn't here. Neither was Daddy. She was alone in the house in the middle of the day and it was fine. She sniffed again. Took the phone from her ear. Sniffed again. It had been that soap. She hadn't noticed it before when she was washing. The fragrance of that sliver of soap sitting unwrapped on the side of the pink sink should have been long gone.

An irritated voice assaulted her, asking if it would be cash or card.

"Sorry, sorry. Card." Where had her mind been just that moment? "Forty minutes? Cool."

That smell of flowers. A fragrance that always reminded her of Mama. A smell she wanted away from. Why did everything have to smell like flowers? Maxine tried to open the window in the half-bathroom, to rid herself of the cloying fragrance, but it wouldn't budge. What had they done to this house?

This place held the memories of Daddy before. When he would rage, Mama would hold Max, cuddling her in her room to keep her from being scared, her coltish legs too long to fit on her lap. She rocked Max back and forth, whispering. "I'm not gonna let you get no man like him. Okay, baby? We're gonna get you a good one. All right?"

Bless her, Mama had tried to no avail. Finally, she had given up, turned to other hobbies of collecting stamps and butterflies. Sometimes, she'd even match them up, pinning the bug to the same card as the stamp, noting the region of both.

On his good days, his recovering days, Daddy was a shell of his formerly angry self and Max could only be grateful. He never talked about those fear-filled times. He just expected to move on to now, never accepting responsibility for his actions when she challenged him.

That was so long ago. I don't even know if I said those things.

I told you that you did, Pop.

Well, I don't remember. How I can apologize for what I don't remember?

How could he not remember following her on her first date with Oscar Ayers, down to the public park and dragging her off the bench they shared as they fed peas to the ducks? Dragging her home and shouting how dirty she was for letting a boy touch her 'tween the legs. She screamed at him that he didn't touch her at all, they had been feeding the ducks and talking, but he was in full rage now, shoving her in the bathtub and filling it with hot water.

"You smell. Wash yourself. Scrub his hands off you." He tossed a bar of soap at her and it hit her shoulder before clattering into the tub. He scrambled in the medicine cabinet while her mother tried to add cool water to the bath. "And use these if you gonna be stink like that."

He'd thrown the box on the lid of the toilet then stormed out of the bathroom. A moment later the door to his and Mama's bedroom slammed. Mama helped Max out of her clothes, then left her to wash in the steaming water while she brought a clean nightgown and underwear. While Mama was gone, she climbed out of the tub and picked up the box, the individual foil-wrapped packets inside rattling, snake-like.

Max's hands moved of their own accord, sliding the door to the mirrored medicine cabinet in the pink bathroom open. The box was still there, as she had somehow known it would be. The floral scent in the bathroom grew, choking her, and she gagged, tasting it.

Fleeing to the back door, Maxine dragged in breath. Years of living alone had kept her from being too casual with her privacy and standing outside on the back porch was a better, safer way to air the house. Get her head and her wits back. She was tired, that was all. From the drive and from the bullshit dealing with the District of Columbia and their police who left her on the floor of that bodega bleeding as they stepped over her. Maxine flipped the snub deadbolt lock and flung the back door wide to find a rainforest jungle.

The description was not far off. As far as she could see was covered in long grasses bent in half from their length, dead dried grasses and shrubs. Barren trees, devoid of flowers or buds. Any fences that separated this property were obscured by vines, and creeping things and the only way she could tell where the border of the property lay was by memory. A weight settled itself on her shoulders.

Could she attack this? Where would she even begin? Hay-like mounds of tree limbs and cast-off leaves were surely turning to compost underneath the piled detritus and vegetation. It was an enormous job. Likely Mister Green only cut the front lawn because he had to walk past it every day and it was easier than complaining about the sight of a property going to pot. Maybe if she paid him enough, he would take care of the back yard before leaving to go to his new condo and his new life, leaving her to stew in hers.

SIX

Sated with pizza and a dose of medicine, Max lounged on the sofa, sighing as the pain began to ease. Not entirely gone, it was still a welcome relief, similar to watching a difficult guest pack their things, knowing that soon they'll be on their way. From where she rested, leg up, she could see the jungle outside. Leaning her head back on the arm of the sofa, she groaned before deciding she should get up and do something with the tangle, clear her mind.

But whenever Max gardened, she ended up spilling blood. It had all been her own—a scrape against thistle left a line of ruby on her brown skin, fine as a spider web. The prick of a rosebud thorn had once brought a shiny sphere of blood to her fingertip. In her first apartment on her own, a moment of carelessness with her secateurs separated the soft flesh between her thumb and forefinger with a chilling *shthop*. She'd run inside, trailing red raindrops from her wound onto the flagstones of the shared garden, back to her apartment.

She'd needed stitches, three of them, to close the cut and she accepted the stern warning from the wall-eyed doctor who'd sewn her up without comment. For two weeks, she watched the skimmia japonica grow wild and the ivy overtake her young cherry tree while she sipped on peppermint tea and seethed. Finally, she hadn't been able to take any more and had donned a thick glove on her stitched hand and forded out to the garden again.

Today, she didn't have gloves and the clearing was slow-going. Panting after only a few minutes of tugging at the overgrown brambles, she returned to the house, promising to do more once she found something to protect her hands. Once it was all done, she could plant some forget-me-nots or foxglove to attract hummingbirds and bees. That big alder shrub had to be pruned and if she left it any longer, she'd have twice the work. And this house needed enough work already.

She gripped the branch close to the trunk of the skimmia with her gloved hand, and snipped it off with the pruning shears using her good hand. After each clip, she yanked the offending branch away, tossing it to a growing pile in the middle of the weed-filled garden. The watery sun overhead gave warmth for a few hours, then cloud cover loomed, taking away the heat of the afternoon. Her back ached, and her healing skin held a pulling itch that said it was time to stop, but she was determined to complete this today. Another few snips and she pulled a huge leafy branch free to reveal a cage.

What was it doing here?

The cage was shoulder height next to her and looked sturdy, but rusted to a crushed velvet brown-bronze. Inside lay a large pile of richly-patterned cloth, scarves or a blanket, maybe. The retreating sun stroked the fabric, turning its deep jewel tones into sparkling metallics. Maxine could just reach the edge of the cloth, somehow untouched by the elements.

Her wiggling fingertips grazed the fabric as she reached through the bars. It was warm, silky. Her face pressed against the crusted bars, trying to get that millimeter closer, when the fabric rustled.

There was no wind today, so it took Maxine a moment to think of what could be moving the pile.

When the pile flipped over, she yanked her hand back with a shriek. Propelled backward, she landed hard on her generous bottom with a grunt of surprise. Right in the one patch of mud in the garden. She cursed.

The man in the cage was regarding her when she looked up. He wrapped the shimmering cloth around himself.

"Hello there," he said.

Maxine screamed, jerking awake on the sofa in the living room of the house on Sans Souci. Her hands shook and when she looked at them, a fine sheen of silvery powder coated her fingertips. She glanced at her phone. 6:17. Was it the a.m. or the p.m.? She didn't know how long she'd slept. Her mouth was dry, like she'd had more than her share of drinks, but only once had she done that. Went out with some work acquaintances and had a few too many. Some good-looking guy saw her at the bar, and before he could say anything, she spouted off about how she was stronger than she looked and she could knock someone out. The guy hightailed it away and her work friends giggled, but didn't invite her out again. Or maybe it was her own humiliation after the fact that made her keep her distance from them for the remainder of her time with the company.

Movement outside the window caught her attention. Groggy, she couldn't figure out what it was. She'd thought it was a person in the back yard. But the movement was there and gone so fast that it couldn't have been. She sat forward, careful of her hip and leg. Peered into the growing darkness. Wind moving all of those trees, branches and whatever else was out there in that yard. A mess. She vowed to tackle it tomorrow.

After finding the house empty, she needed to take her own break from things and do something physical. That was what she had liked about her most recent job. It was moving, lifting, doing, and it helped keep her mind out of the spaces it shouldn't be. Those deep pockets of memory that could sink an entire day in misery and self-pity were pitfalls she wanted, needed, to avoid. It was hard to do sometimes. Being back in the house where they happened, even harder.

The smell of the leftover pizza was making her ill. She closed the lid and headed for the trash can. But she had no desire to go back out to get food, so instead she shoved the entire box in the fridge. She filled her travel cup with water from the tap, guzzled it down, rivers rolling down her cheeks.

She wiped the water from her face, and leaned against the counter in the kitchen. What the hell was going on in this house? She felt like a child again, like she had when Daddy had forgotten that Mama was staying overnight at the hospital after her hysterectomy. He had gone out somewhere—God knew where—and Max had come home from school, tired, frustrated that she couldn't find any friends who wanted to sit with her after Daddy's tirade a few weeks ago in her teacher's room. Over the rule that whoever picked her up at school had to be on the list.

Uncle Ronnie, one of Daddy's old military buddies, wasn't on the list and had been turned away from picking her up. Daddy had been in no shape to see people, but he had made his drunk ass way down to the school and ranted and raved until Mama was able to get off from her day job and pick them both up. Mama had been let go from the day job and Daddy had given Max the reputation that she and her family were not to be trusted.

On that day, Max had come trekking through the rising flood waters and pouring rain to find the house empty. "Daddy?" she'd called. For some reason she rationalized that Daddy must be at the hospital with Mama and would be home soon. The house was without family noise, and it was the kind of frightening when something familiar is suddenly strange. The paralyzing kind of fright where you don't know what to do, so you do nothing. Max stood in the middle of the hallway, dripping water for a good few minutes until it hit her: she would help out.

After shucking her raincoat into the bathroom to dry, she grabbed a towel to mop up the water she'd left in her wake. Mama had left a pre-made dish wrapped in foil in the fridge for Daddy to heat up for dinner while she was away overnight. Max read the note:

Oven on 350.
Heat for 20 min with the foil on.

Max could do that. On tiptoe, she turned the oven to the correct temperature. The ceramic tray was heavier than she'd expected but she managed it, pushing it to the back of the oven. She didn't know how to set the timer on the oven, but she could tell time on the brass wall clock; knew how to read the slowly creeping hands. It was hard, waiting. And so boring. She ran upstairs to change out of her damp school clothes and into dry play clothes but that only took four minutes. Then she turned on the radio; TV wasn't allowed before dinner during the week. It was okay, because they ate like old people around four o'clock in the afternoon.

She danced to the sounds of Mama's disco, hustling left and right, squealing when she missed a step and rushing to start over. She slid along the kitchen floor in her socks, making the slick moves easier for her clumsy footwork. Nowhere near the moves she saw on reruns of *Soul Train* on Saturday mornings, when she and Mama cleaned the house, but it wasn't too bad. Max was breathless after about four songs, and she looked up at the clock. It was time to take the dinner out. She yanked the oven door open—too hard—and it bounced back up, closing with a ringing, metallic thud. Max let out a tiny shriek, and twisted away from its path.

Using the ladybug-printed oven mitts hanging on the oven door, she opened it more carefully this time. Leaning deep into the oven was a feeling she'd never felt before. Like the hottest summer ever, choking heat that didn't let up, until she could hardly breathe. It was like trying to suck in hot, meaty wind. She grasped the side of the casserole dish and scuttled away from the oven like a frightened crab.

Scared crabs get tough, Maxie, Mama had said once while she was making this same dish. *Put them in the fridge so they go to sleep. It's easier to kill them that way and their meat doesn't toughen up.*

Deep breath of hot air and she gathered her strength to lift the dish. Up, up and onto the stove eye. She nudged the oven closed with her foot. Remembered to turn it off. Max couldn't recall a moment in all her seven years where she'd felt more accomplished.

But the hands of the clock kept moving and Max continued to be alone in the house. No one came home. She called the hospital but at the sound of her voice, the short patience nurse told her to stop playing on the phone and hung up. The music on the radio turned to the old, old stuff she didn't like as much and she turned it off. TV kept her company as she ate the cooling crab rice from her Wonder Woman cereal bowl while images on the screen flickered across her vision. She didn't recall what she'd watched, but it was noise to cover the sounds of the house that seemed to know she was alone. There were more noises than usual, weren't there? More creepy sounds and creaks.

Max crept to the kitchen and covered the rest of the food up with foil. She didn't want any more; she wanted a dessert. Something sweet would fill that empty part of her, the part that was kinda scared, kinda excited about being home alone. She knew she wasn't supposed to be, but she had no idea where Daddy was and more calls to the hospital were no help. She settled back on the couch with a sleeve of cookies and a blanket.

She must have fallen asleep at some point, because when she woke up the TV was blaring some kind of alert. Max sat up in the darkness and stared at the screen, her fingers in her ears to try and cull the noise. It had been light when she'd fallen asleep. A countdown had begun on the TV... to what she didn't know. 4... 3... 2...

At one, the screen changed to static. A black, white, and gray hiss that sounded like a warning.

You're alone, little girl. In this house.

Alone with me.

Alone with the house.

Inside me.

Max burrowed deeper into the couch. Her mind screamed, *Go to bed,* but she could not get up. Couldn't get up to turn the TV off. They didn't have one of those new TVs with the remote control. They had one of Daddy's old ones that he kept repairing. She would have to go over to the screen and turn the dial until it clicked off. No... No, she couldn't do that.

The static hissed, taunting her.

Come here. Reach out to me...

Max covered her head with the blanket. Grasped one of the couch cushions and pulled it onto her face. If she couldn't see it coming, it would be okay.

It would be okay if it got her. As long as she didn't see it.

The next thing Max knew, it was morning and the news was on the TV. A bright shining morning and a smiling man was telling her the temperature outside. Sunny today, maybe to help dry up all that rain we had yesterday and into last night. Enjoy the sunshine, folks!

Slowly, Max pushed the cushion away, sat up, blinking the sleep from her eyes. What time was it? Morning. But what—

The front door opened, and a figure appeared in the doorway. Hunched, hobbling, it made its way inside. Max stood up, ready to bolt if she had to. Or hide. Maybe hiding was better. She crept backwards, hoping to find a place before—

Her foot hit the half-eaten sleeve of cookies and it crinkled, explosion-loud in the quiet of the house. The figure turned, gasped. Shuffled in further. Then—

"Maxie, baby? That you?"

"Mama!"

She ran to her for a hug, weak with relief, only to have her gasp at the contact. "I'm sorry."

"It's okay, baby. Let Mama sit down. Where's your daddy?"

Little Max said nothing. Mama's hand gripped hers firmer, led her to the couch. "Did you sleep down here?"

A nod.

"What about dinner?"

"I heated the food you left for us."

"In the oven?"

"Yes," she whispered.

After a few minutes Mama got the entire story out of Max and still no Daddy. He came home around lunchtime and after eating, her parents disappeared behind a closed door. She thought she remembered shouting, and wanting to turn the TV back on to drown it out, but it had betrayed her too. By becoming a fearful thing, by changing into something to be afraid of. Instead, she climbed into bed next to the rest of the cookies she'd sneaked up and ate until she felt better. Pressing her tongue to the crumbs on the sheets, she thought, *Soon. Soon it'll be quiet and I can go to sleep.*

Later that night when hunger struck, she tiptoed down to the kitchen, using the meager light from the open fridge to peer out of the back window. Silence ruled over the garden and she was able to see little besides the gentle wind rustling the taller branches of the plum and apple trees silhouetted against the gray night. Even so, she didn't feel alone.

SEVEN

In her parent's bedroom, Max found her old diary, one she'd forgotten she'd even had. Powder blue with pink lined pages and a tiny lock. There was no key, but it looked like the lock had been pried open anyway. She eased herself down on their four poster bed and read.

November 3, 1994

I think Daddy is so mean because he wants us to prove that we will love him no matter what. He gets to be so awful to us and we have to still love him and keep him around. We have to accept that he is angry and be gracious and tell him we understand and that it's okay for him to be angry at us because the world is so angry at men and black men. And we have to soak up all his anger like a sponge so he is free of it and after we have to hold it inside us until we dry out and become hard.

Also like sponges.

December 18, 1994

I think Daddy feels that now he has a kid, he can treat me the way he was treated when he was my age. He doesn't have the idea that Now I have a child, I want my child to have a better life than I did. No, he feels like: I got through my childhood. You will get through yours. You'll survive.

Maybe I shouldn't say he feels this way. I'm not sure Daddy feels. At all.

Maxine put down the diary. She was choking on it, on her own words, coming back at her through time like a sci-fi movie scientist on a mission to save humanity. But this was all wrong and time was flowing the wrong way. She was in the future, and it was her that should be going back to the past to save her younger self, not the other way around. Just showed how wrong those movies could be.

~~Febu~~ February 10, 1995

We have to be perfect or he gets angry. We can't make mistakes or have a bad day or just forget or anything. We can't be people. We must be perfect all the time. Mama says it's impossible to me later, after Daddy is asleep. We can't be perfect little butterflies, beautiful and delicate. They do not live long.

Personal days. Mama has lots of them at work, but she won't take any. I'd rather be at work than here when Daddy's home.

She recalled her first time. How stunned she'd been when she realized the pain she'd thought was needing to go to the bathroom wasn't. When she'd pulled down her underwear, a clot wobbled like soft-set gelatin atop the white cotton gusset, a self-created objet d'art. There was no emotion in her, only the wooden movement of tipping the clot into the porcelain bowl, and the echoing sound of it hitting the bottom.

"Mama!"

Mama must have heard something in her voice and came to the bathroom. Thankfully. She didn't always, her default being that Max, as the child, should come to her. A sign of respect for her time and for her position. It was only later that Max realized that people who demand their titles, demand respect, sometimes do so because it has been so long denied them.

Max leaned forward to unlock the door. Delight and worry twisted her mother's fine features. Her voice was gentle as if coaxing a frightened puppy.

"You okay. It happens. Remember we talked about it?"

Max nodded, the scent of copper in her nostrils, pain corkscrewing through her abdomen and lower belly.

"I'll get you some clean panties, then you can use the napkins, okay? I'll show you."

Daddy came up behind Mama before she could close the door. He didn't ask what was happening, just scanned the room, seeing the blood and abstract art. His lip curled, and he wrinkled his wide nose, sucked his teeth.

He pointed at her with an unlit cigarette between his first two fingers. "Why'd you have to go and get that? I don't wanna see none of that stuff, hear? I don't wanna know when you got it." His footsteps resounded on the dark hardwood floor as he stomped away down the hall toward the front door. Ignoring her pleas for him to understand that she didn't mean to, that she was sorry, that she didn't want to upset him, but—

He grabbed his jacket off the chair near the door. "Just don't bring no babies in this house." The hinges rattled when he slammed the door.

Mama returned, silent as the grave to hand her clean underwear and take away the soiled ones. Daddy didn't return until long past her bedtime.

The bleeding was so much, too much by her mother's account. Each month, she was exhausted, but there was no break in her schedule of school and working part-time. Daddy had gone upstate to Columbia to get a special request to allow her to work, even though the laws said she had to be sixteen and that would be another year from now. The state granted it with no issue; Daddy could be charming when he wanted to be, especially with people outside the family.

One day when she came home, he didn't look up when he sniffed the air and said, "I can smell you, gal. Go take a bath." She was tired, overheated from all day at school, the bus ride to work, and the walk home afterwards. She hadn't had much to drink and all she wanted was some water and a chance to sit down. But at the look on his face she knew better than to sit her body on one of the chairs. One of his chairs. It was awful to know that she caused her father, a beautiful man, by all the women at church's standard, to have his face so twisted with anger it was ugly.

Max was so exhausted by the day she'd had that she'd stood and stared at him while he got angrier and angrier until Mama jumped up and grabbed her arm. "I'll run the water for you, baby. Come on. I'll use those bubbles you like."

She took the bath, using the special soap Daddy bought for her and Mama. Towel wrapped under her arms, she glanced away from her reflection and opened the medicine cabinet. Took the box of foil-wrapped packages and opened it, tore one free of the line. She split the foil and removed the item inside.

It was a shaped like a pyramid, squashed to almost flat from the sides. Spring Garden, it was called, the fragrance. It engulfed her, intensifying as the scented wax tablet warmed in her fingers. She'd put one foot up on the closed toilet lid and inserted it between her legs.

When Max came back to the present, she was laying on her bed, the diary open and face down next to her. She thought there was someone standing there, nestled in the corner of the room like a shadow. But it was only another stain, this one ran almost to the ceiling, well above her own height. Daylight made her brave, the sun beating everything into submission outside as good as a belt of liquor to strengthen her nerves. Maxine approached the stain like it was a stranger she wanted to know, with curiosity and a touch of chagrin. The stain was like an oil painting, with raised layers of texture. Some softened parts of the drywall had gotten wet, and sunk in slightly, then re-hardened to a valley her fingers found irresistible to press. The peaks of the stain were small, sharp mountains that pricked at her fingertips, as though promising slumber.

Max wondered why she was touching something that was in all probability growing mold along the wall. Mister Green was right. The house needed work, and she wasn't helping matters. Suppose she'd pressed the wall and it had crumbled in, releasing a miasma of throat destroying spores. She pulled her hand away, let it head for her jeans, but just short of wiping away the mold she stopped and strode to the bathroom. No telling what that muck was. It was better if she washed her hands. Nothing to do with Daddy. The soap's floral scent strengthened as she lathered the bar and scrubbed her hands, fragrance rising into the air like smoke after an explosion. Smell hung in the room, sticking to Max's tongue as she swallowed the perfume down, choking on its beauty.

Tariq called. He hadn't talked to her since the accident, hadn't returned her messages saying that she was going to seek legal rep. She'd thought he'd ghosted her, and he had. But for some reason she would always be grateful for, he sent a copy of their conversation to her attorney, who used the information to get her a settlement. Some of the money had gone to the attorney, but most to her medical bills.

Max eased her hip into a more comfortable position on the bed. "I'm in bed for the night. What do you want, Tariq? I haven't heard from you since—"

"I know, but look," he started, and she could almost see him in her mind's eye, rubbing a hand over his mouth before talking. His tell that he was lying. But she had little to do here and since the garden had bested her today, she wanted something she could control. "I sent that tape, right?"

"Yeah, you did. I never got a chance to thank you for that."

"So thank me, girl. Thank me."

She chuckled, unable to deny that he had for a time brought something important into her life. If not joy, distraction. Yes, it had ended and she had sat alone in her apartment recovering for months. But he had given her something there too. He'd given her a person to hate and that had been the best fuel to get up each day and work her knotted muscles and massage the keloided flesh into some suppleness. She had imagined his face, with its sparse taco-meat beard, and being able to stride up to it and slap the smirk off of it into next week.

But now, alone in the house, it was easy to fall back into patterns. Late-night calls or texts when Tariq got in from whereever he said he had been, her believing but not believing him, and choosing the easy way of interacting: pretending everything was cool when she wanted something more.

Don't have expectations, Max, don't want things. Then they can't deny you those things. Because that hurts so much more.

"I appreciate you, Tariq."

"You know I got you."

She shook her head. "Nope, I don't know that."

"Maxine," he said, drawing the word out in way she hated. It wheedled, trying to be coaxing, seductive, but sounding like a child wanting forgiveness without having to give an apology.

When she didn't respond, he was quiet for a moment. "You gotta understand… I just couldn't see you like that. Don't act like I don't give a shit about you. I'm here now."

"And I'm 500 miles away."

"Word? You left without saying nothin."

"I stayed trying to contact you, Tariq, but you didn't ever answer. I had to leave."

"Uh. So you don't need me no more."

She hadn't ever needed him, not really, until the accident and he'd evaporated like so much dew under sunlight. That was his issue, honestly. That she didn't need him as much as he wanted to be needed. Question was, did she want him now? Did she need him now… even if it was only to assuage the loneliness and the fill the swollen silence that living in this house brought.

Max blew out a breath, giving him credit for a seduction he hadn't performed. "Tell you what I do need."

His victory snicker almost lost it for him. She wanted to be taken seriously, especially now. She wanted him to listen, to take her needs and wants into consideration, not the respect of his friends from the job that he'd invited over to play cards.

No, that wasn't Tariq, that was Daddy.

She pulled the covers up over herself, shaking off the skin of that thought, dragging Tariq closer for an experience that would wipe out the ones wriggling in her head like bugs sprayed with insecticide. Like she had done so many times in the past, she lowered her voice into a whisper to let him know she was ready to waste her time with him.

"What you got for me? What you wearin?"

When she told him she was wearing a t-shirt and her underwear, he laughed. A full on from-the-belly laugh that set her jaw and her teeth on edge. "Pannies? What you wearing pannies to bed for? You worried about ghosts?"

She turned over onto her belly, protecting her softest parts. Yes, that was exactly what she was worried about.

EIGHT

When she was a senior in high school, she'd tried to get Mama to leave Daddy. She'd read enough to know this was abuse in such a sinister form. Divorce him, get out. He won't change. Ever, no matter what you did for him.

All she would say was she was working on it.

"Working on him or working on leaving?" Max had asked.

"Working on him."

"Mama, you need to go."

"I know," she'd whispered. Max could picture her in her housedress, twirling the yellow phone cord around and around in her fingers. "I will. When you have a break, like over Christmas, I'll do it then, so you can help me."

She'd wanted Mama to stand up and leave on her own. Why didn't she want to preserve herself? Save herself. Resentment over having to be there simmered in Max and she thought about not staying home for Christmas break. Force Mama to do it herself. But she knew she wouldn't... not without her there.

People don't change.

On the final day before Christmas Break something had changed. Max was looking forward to spending it with her mother alone, just the two of them talking about the fragile memories of the good times and discussing how they could make the future better for them both. Max was employed, Mama was too. If they shared a small apartment, they could make it work. One bedroom was fine. She would sleep on the couch while Mama had the bedroom. She'd need the space for her drawing.

But when she'd got home from a long day at school and a shift at the home goods store, the house was decorated for Christmas. People milled around inside the house and because of the mild winter, the front and back porches. Cousins, godparents, church siblings... all festive dress, laughing and partying. Daddy in the back with the grill on. The scent of fire and ash in the crisp air. The press of bodies in the house was crushing, overwhelming her with the smells of freshly pressed hair and barber shop talc.

It took ages to find her mother and drag her away from her guests to a private corner. She had to control her anger enough to ask with a modicum of calm in her voice, "Mama, what happened? I thought we were going to get you out of here when I got home? It was supposed to be the two of us, getting a new place and getting your things together..."

"Not this time, it's Christmas." She smiled and waved at someone Max didn't know, her face beatific, eyes distant as they gazed over the revelers. "Isn't it nice?"

Max shook her head hard, the burned ends of her braids striking the tender skin of her cheeks, scratching them. "I feel like I'm going crazy. What is happening here?"

"Ain't nothin wrong with crazy." She blinked, hurt in her raised voice. "Can't I just have something? My whole family around for Christmas like we used to have?"

That was when Max noticed Daddy had set out all the old holiday decorations Gramma and Granddad had used. She remembered so little about them, except for Mama's stories of their legendary parties that went on into the wee hours of the night. Kids in bed early, everyone dressed to the nines, dancing until dizzy. The record player was spinning a scratchy old record. Max watched the red vinyl go around and around, the crooner's words holding her in their thrall.

While fields and floods, rocks, hills and plains
Repeat the sounding joy
Repeat the sounding joy
Repeat, repeat, the sounding joy

Max could still hear the lyrics to the carol, as she gazed outside at the back yard again. Then they'd been able to have guests and parties out there on the manicured lawn. No longer.

Huddled masses of hay-like weeds dominated the entire area, giving it an enclosed, womb-like feeling. Tentacles of ivy choked what was once her mother's prized garden. Raised planting beds that used to be home to rows of vegetables—tomatoes, okra, onions, kale—were filled with dusty soil crawling with dandelion leaves. The loquat tree Max used to climb as a child was bare of fruit and blossoms. What was once a path through the back yard to the potting shed where Mama used to do her sketching, now was covered over in sun-bleached grass. Someone at some time had tried to keep the mass controlled, dead grasses and brambles lay in crispy-looking mounds on one side of the yard, piled high as her head.

Even with the overgrown garden, the area was empty of life. February was usually temperate enough here to allow something to grow, but there was no activity of any kind. Without the chirrup of birds, the hum of bees, or even the annoying buzz of mosquitoes— the silence in the back yard was an echo of the silence that emerged after the gunshot at the bodega. The world around her had fallen silent for unknown moments, or maybe it was her own ears, unable to pick up any sound.

It had been part of what had kept her lying on that filthy floor in that bodega, clutching her phone in a sweat-slick grip. Even Tariq's face on the screen had blurred out for a moment, as she soaked in her blood and pain. Her body had slowed. Each blink an eternity between them, as she watched the silence react to the world around it. It had become its own person, a creature, really. Moving through the store, looking for victims to cover with itself. Unable to vocalize, Max felt her mouth moving, felt the push of air through her lungs, but didn't know if she was even speaking. Another slow blink, another eternity. Then finally, footsteps.

Leaving home so soon after school was over had been a kind of frightening freedom. No one was going to bother her for things, but no one was gonna be there for her either. All of that made for a strange vacancy inside herself that she could fill with anything and all the choice in the world was too much. She couldn't settle, couldn't decide for more than a few months at a time on what she wanted to do with her new life away from the house and the family.

She'd spent some time waitressing at a 24-hour diner, and moved up to manager within a few months. More out of the diner's necessity that any real acumen on her part. She left soon after, because she hated being responsible for the staff: the scheduling, the payment, the discipline. She hated being the one customers complained to about workers who were just trying to make a living and she didn't care that their bread was too toasted or that the heat from the burger made their lettuce leaf limp. So she'd moved on to another job. And another and another. Until she finally had to stay somewhere in order to not have a hard time finding employment. That was when she'd met Tariq.

He was on shift with her at Duppy Shack, a pan-Caribbean restaurant in D.C. It suited her more to be there, allowed to say they had no more of something without apologizing. You should get here earlier, is what Anne-Marie told her to say to anyone who complained. *We don' accept nunna dat talk.* She shrugged her shoulders, bare arms glistening in the heat of the kitchen. *We run out, we run out. What we guh do?*

Tariq had told her that attitude was what saved him. "You can't save nobody but yourself, can you? Telling customers like it is, man... that is life right there." He took a drag off a rollie, blew out a thin steam of smoke. "I don't have to worry about nobody telling me I gotta be nice. Customer ain't always right. Who came up with that bullshit?"

She didn't stay at Duppy Shack long; she and Tariq got caught messing around too much for that, but she had fallen into a delivery job that paid better, and had good benefits.

Maxine shook off the memory, rubbed the back of her neck with her palm. God, she was tired. She turned away from the back door to head deeper into the house's embrace for a nap. She lived here now, whether Daddy was going to like it or not. She'd tell him like it was when he got home. If he got home. If he didn't, she would report him missing. Start the clock that would soon make the house hers.

And just in time, because she had nowhere else.

NINE

It was too hot in the bedroom. Too hot in the house. Unable to rest, Maxine fidgeted in bed, the sweat on her skin making her feel slick and dirty. She fought the urge to get up and shower, even though it would make her feel cooler. So hot, it drained her of all energy, made her feel faint. She kicked off the thin percale sheet with her good leg, even its light weight was making it ache, adding to the heat in her body.

She stretched the offending limb out, pointed, then flexed her foot, wiggled her toes. Rarely did she do her physio exercises anymore, but now the routine would help focus her mind. She moved more easily through the series of stretching exercises, breathing deeply and slowly. Where had Mama gone? She understood why she left Daddy, but where was she now? No online searches for Genevieve Forest had produced any results. Tomorrow, she'd try again. Maybe find someone to look at the house for the mold situation. That must be where these strange dreams had been coming from. It was possible it was some sort of hallucinogen? People died from mold spore inhalation, didn't they?

Maxine placed both soles of her feet on the mattress, pulled her heels as close to her butt as she could. A bright, sparking tightness in her lower right abdomen arced into her right hip and outer thigh. Her legs wouldn't go back any more, so she grasped her ankles and pulled them another fraction of an inch. She hissed with the pain, then as it receded into a mild burn, she sighed, satisfied.

She let go of her ankles, flinging her arms out wide and let her knees fall open, releasing a wave of floral perfume from her fabric-covered slit. It felt good to be this open. The window unit air conditioner cycled on again, lifting the corner of the sheet. Hardening her nipples. Finally, she slept as something else awakened. Roiled in an ecstasy of its own awareness of her presence. Delighted, it began to move.

Max woke close to orgasm, her heart thudding in her chest, her mind bewildered as to where she could be to be receiving such treatment. But the pleasure slid away from her as she woke, evaporating like an alarm-broken dream. Her flesh tried to clutch at the sensation, to keep the fleeing sensation inside, but it was gone. All that was left was the agony in her hip from leaving her legs open so long.

After a vicious curse, she struggled up from the bed and padded to the bathroom. When she sat on the toilet, she saw small holes in the gusset of her underwear.

"What the—"

They were small tears as if someone tore them with the point of a pencil. She hadn't noticed after taking them out of the dryer. "Great. Another thing I need to buy. It'll have to wait. No one's going to see them."

She tossed the underwear in the trash and headed for the shower. On her mental to-do list, she added: *Call a mold removal specialist* to *Go to the bank* and *Get groceries*.

The shock of the air-conditioned air of TruNational hitting her sweat-damp skin made Maxine shudder.

"Are you okay?"

Concern lay in the voice of the bank employee who approached her but not in the older woman's face. That was carefully composed into a professional mask she'd likely been wearing a long time.

"I'm fine." Max dropped her sunglasses into her purse. "I need to get into a safe deposit box."

"Name?"

"Genevieve and Maxine Forest."

The name must have been a trigger for the woman. Her mouth tightened, twitched, then opened slowly, like the portcullis to Dracula's castle. Or a woman who has had to always choose her words.

"That box—"

"I can pay it up to date. Then close it out." Max finished the words, crisply. She didn't want any issues, only to get the stuff and go. "How much is it?"

"Two hundred-sixty dollars."

Maxine gaped. "You don't need to check… on the computer or something?"

"No, ma'am." The woman motioned her over to a desk anyway, sat, and began typing. "I send out all the letters for overdue boxes, and not many get to the abandoned property stage. But I'll show you."

It struck Max that she was no longer used to hearing the honorific. She stayed standing, about to say she wasn't old enough to have that word directed at her until she realized it was silly. It had nothing to do with age. It was a sign of respect, no different than using an honorific in a language like Japanese or Burmese. Still, her lips twisted, holding back a sharp response. These banks made money hand over fist and had the nerve to charge people fees for accessing their own money and property.

"Here it is."

Miss I'm-gonna-call-you-ma'am turned her monitor toward Max, folded her hands on the desk. "I'd need to settle this amount before allowing you to access the box." Her posture was rigid, her tone gently neutral. Max recognized it as the reaction of a person used to being yelled at for adhering to a set of rules she'd had no part in making.

"That's fine," she replied, matching the woman's careful tone. "Will you take a debit card?"

"Of course."

"Thank you, Ms…"

"Melody. It's just Melody."

After taking her money and giving her a receipt, Melody let Max into the safety deposit area. She followed her into the recesses of the vault housing the endless rows of steel boxes, where the air was stale with a metallic tang. As a kid, she'd loved coming here, going beyond the vault door had felt like entering a portal to another world. Now she could see it for what it was: a stuffy, enclosed space that hadn't been well-cared for because it was seen to be strong enough to not need maintenance. Confining. The carpet was ancient, what little light there was reflected off the pewter-hued boxes lining the vault floor to ceiling.

"Number 236."

Melody took a set of keys that hung on her waist and pulled the cord taut to select a key. She inserted it in one of the two keyholes at the front of the drawer, then looked expectantly at Max.

"Sorry. I should have had this out." She dug in her bag, down the middle and into the side pockets. "I know it's in here—ow!"

Max jerked her finger out of her bag. "What the hell was that?" It felt like a needle prick, one that had gone under her nailbed but there was nothing in her bag that could have caused it. She pressed her thumbnail against the hurt, but no blood welled. Why the hell did it hurt that much, then? Shit.

Gingerly, she resumed her search and found the small red envelope easily this time and pulled it free with a tenuous grip. Pushed it into the lock. This part, she remembered. She and Melody exchanged glances, then turned their keys at the same time. The locks tumbled, released. Melody opened the door and extracted the drawer inside and handed it over, indicating the private viewing room with an opened palm.

Max locked herself inside the stark room, that held nothing but a desk and a chair, feeling like some kind of thief with a haul of illegal goods. The cold metal and plastic of the chair bit into the skin of her back and thighs. Finally, an answer to the one thing she couldn't seem to remember: what was in the box. She lifted the hinge and flipped the lid open.

Sugar cubes in pale hues of sick—yellow, purple, blue—each one pasted on a slip of card with pencil markings under each, the lead too faded to read.

Polaroids of wooded areas, none she recognized. Mostly close ups of some bushes and woodland.

Small vials, the size of generous perfume samples. Whatever liquid they held had long since dried out.

Deposit slips and bank statements.

An envelope

She took out the bank statements first. Mama had been putting away part of her check from the scientist for years. If it were anyone else, she would have cheered her on her plans to break free of such an abusive husband. But this was her mother and she couldn't help the anger and betrayal that flared up. She'd kept money away from the family. Money she could have used to help Max to go on a school trip or get a new backpack or anything that would have kept her from being so singled out as a kid. No, that was unfair. Mama had given her money that allowed Max to flee. She was beginning to think it wasn't the house taking her back to places she didn't want to revisit, but the entire city.

No, no. She wasn't going to fall into victim blaming. Terror makes us cruel. One day, she needed to look up who said that or wrote that. Maybe the knowledge would help her process the fear Mama had labored under. She dumped the statements back in the box and removed the envelope.

More photos. These were in their own fold over sleeve, indicating they had been sent to a photo development place or been hand-developed by someone who knew how. Each photo was close-up and glossy, detailing the outer and inner images of various insects. Intact in the first picture of its kind, the subsequent photos showed the bugs precisely flayed apart, revealing the delicate systems that moved these creatures.

Then, she removed an artist's sketchbook, several pages at the beginning had been cut or pulled out cleanly. As she flipped through the remaining sheets of archival paper, she realized what she'd found. Some of Mama's drawings for the scientist she'd worked for.

They'd littered the dining room table when Max was growing up: these perfect diagrams of the glossy photos. Some in grayscale done with pencil, lined with a trickle of black ink, others in rich hues that showed the brilliance of the insects' various patterns and shades.

These scientific illustrations were how Mama had supported the family when Daddy hadn't been able to hold onto his job. Max looked closer, seeing the intricacies her mother had been able to duplicate. Innards looked slick, wet. Mouth parts gaping and cavernous showed concentric circles of teeth, fading into the darkness of some unknown maw. Skin crawling, she flicked to the next sheet of paper.

Labeled "Rhopolocera", this image was from above, showing the butterfly's wings open to reveal a shimmering pattern of black and green and yellow. Next to the spread wings drawing was another: a cross-section revealing its inner workings. Each minuscule part was labeled:

Cerebral ganglion

Salivary gland

Testis

Esophagus

Hearts

"Hearts?" Max whispered. In the enclosed, empty space her whisper echoed, coming back to her like a punishment. Hadn't Mama said something about that once? Two hearts, for the wings.

She stared at the drawings a little longer, flipping through all of them again. At the sight of the ants, the crickets, she shook her head, then closed the cover of the sketchbook. To her disappointment, nothing in here was incriminating. Part of her had hoped this box had contained something clandestine like counterfeit bills, or some illegal drugs, or the weapon Mama had used to kill Daddy and bury him in the back yard.

So Mama had just left, then. Max closed the empty box after shoving everything into a plastic bag, then into her purse. More than ever she wanted to talk to her mother and find out how, after all these years, she'd managed to bring herself to leave. What had been the last straw that made her say, "Enough!" and walk out. Had the years softened Daddy enough that he just let her go?

She went to grasp the empty box, then remembered to zip her bag closed first. Whatever this compilation of stuff was, it was hers to deal with and not for any outside eyes. Hitching her bag on her shoulder, Max went to look for Melody.

TEN

With more than a little hesitation, Max opened the door to her old bedroom. She'd changed it herself over the years, going from unframed, color-saturated boy band posters on her walls to framed Ansel Adams photos, to her own drawings. Botanical drawings appealed most.

She got that from Mom. Mama was an artist, a good one, too— even great, perhaps at one point if she'd been encouraged. Mama's mama thought so little of anything creative that she found chores for her daughter to do instead.

Mama had told Max once that she'd wanted to be an artist for a living, but her own mother hadn't approved.

"You can't make a living off drawing, Genevieve."

"People do. All the time."

"You ain't people. You a woman, and you Black." She scoffed as they folded clothes together. "You need a skill, a job where someone gone give you a regular, steady check. Maybe you can draw if you get a husband who pay your bills. Otherwise…"

"Those words hung in the air like a sword over my neck," Mama told her. "I thought it was the truth. Why not? I trusted my mother to tell me the right thing."

Mama had gotten Daddy for her husband. Married right out of school and things had gone fine for a long while, both of them holding down full-time jobs. Then Max came along and Daddy wanted Mama to stop working and stay home. But he hadn't anticipated how much having a child would change the household, would morph and stretch his wife into being a mother as well. The cost of a baby's care, the noisy nights when she was awake with colic and crying to all hours. Max disrupted the calm of the house and Daddy started going out at night with his friends. Coming home later and later, smelling more and more like the brown liquor he favored.

Soon, he couldn't keep up with the bills and Mama had to find a job again. But the place she'd left didn't want her back, so she had to look elsewhere. Max couldn't remember where Mama had found the advertisement for the scientific illustrator job, but it had been perfect. Getting photos in the mail from some university scientist or researcher or whatever he was, then drawing larger versions, to show all the tiny parts more clearly. Sometimes there were seven or eight photos of one bug, including close-ups and cross-sections. There'd be notes in his scratchy handwriting. *This one black and white. This one must be in full color. Can you label the parts? My penmanship, as you can see, is quite illegible.*

Beautiful butterflies, sturdy beetles, the fuzzy-soft wild bees. Pictures of them intact, pictures of others dissected, their intricate miniature systems displayed for the delectation of the viewer. Occasionally, she would have to speak with him on the phone and she would mention the weird things she learned from her boss.

Did you know butterflies have two hearts? Isn't it amazing? It helps pump blood to their wings.

71

I had no idea there were so many types of bees. Did you, Max?

If Daddy overheard, he would tolerate a few minutes of the conversation as he knew it brought in money they sorely needed. But after he'd been home a while, two or three drinks in, he'd get that growly sound to his voice, start shifting in his chair and Mama would know to stop.

Max loved Mama's stories, she seemed so animated and excited when telling them, but Daddy seethed. He never stopped Mama from working for the man, though. The money was too good. Was he called Dr. No? Max drummed her fingers on the tabletop, thinking. Dr. Novye, that was his name.

One night she'd heard Mama and Daddy arguing. *Don't nobody pay that much to for no drawings. Pictures for chrussake. You sleeping with him? Hm? That what you doing when I'm at work?*

No! He's not like that. He doesn't even live near here.

He sucked his teeth so loud Max could hear the whistle in the hallway. *Whatever, Genevieve. He put his mouth on you. Huh?*

No!

Maxine covered her head with her pillow and tried to drown them out.

You don't want a man like your daddy. I'ma make sure you get someone better.

She chuckled softly. Mama hadn't had the chance to do that. All her time and effort was spent on figuring a way to get Max out of the house. And she had. She'd gotten herself out too, but to where? Was she still drawing for that doctor? Did he help her get out? The thought that Daddy might have been right all along rocked her back in her seat. Was Mama having an affair with the doc?

Grabbing her phone, Maxine headed to the dining room table where she looked up Dr. Noyve's name. Several entries, all of them professional. He must be a busy guy. Smart with all those letters after his name. She headed to the webpage for the Center for Eco

Preservation where he now lectured on insects and how eating them will be the future of food. According to him, they are more plentiful, more sustainable, and just as high in protein as other meats we consume that are less renewable. No matter how smart he was, he wasn't getting her to eat bugs.

He also wasn't handsome, not like Daddy was before the drink, with his wide, white smile and his barrel chest. Dr. Novye looked— indoor, almost delicate. His eyes were wide under his glasses, and he looked… unassuming, maybe even weird. There are more pictures of him bent over a microscope, talking to another white-coated man with a similar lanky build. She clicked on the video link attached to the page and to her surprise his voice belied the rest of his looks. It was clear, authoritative, and it even grabbed her attention as he tried to convince the viewer to eat bugs as a lifestyle change.

He paused to take off his round wire-rimmed glasses. While he polished them on a soft-looking cloth, he stared into the camera. His eyes were pale, piercing in their uncomfortable intensity. "They would eat us if they could. Why not return the favor?"

Max paused the video. Never. Would she eat insects. Not knowingly. But she'd eaten after that butterfly had its sample of her crab dip, hadn't she? So in that case, she was the scavenger, feasting on leftovers. She shuddered, pushing the thought away. Then opened another video.

In this one, people in suits and white coats milled around in the background and she could see the doctor was really tall compared to them, although still painfully thin. He introduced his team, each of them coming forward to smile or nod. Then he looked off camera and she heard a small whispered, "No."

Then after a pause, a whispered "Okay."

The doctor smiled, indulgently. "Let me introduce my assistant, without whom I could get nothing done. G.L. Wood." The look of pure pride on his face made him almost attractive for a moment. Max snorted a laugh that faded as the camera panned over.

"My God. Mama."

After years of not seeing her mother, Max had preserved an image of her in her mind. Frozen in clear ice like some fossil from an Ice Age a millennia ago. An image of her mother as worn, worried, but resolute that her daughter would have a chance. It was the look she had remembered so often on her mother's face and on her body that it had become a statue in her mind. As if she were in a museum and the installation was called, *Doting Mother Under Glass*, weeping, eternally giving. Sacrificing her own flesh for her flesh and blood.

It would have won some award.

But this woman she was seeing now was nothing like *Doting Mother*. She looked amazing. Gone was the timid, fear-filled woman of Max's memory. Where… how? When the letter had arrived, she'd known Mama had left Daddy. That knowledge was reinforced when she got to the house. But how long ago had she left? Max paused the video to stare at the screen. It was her mother, even though the name under the woman's picture wasn't. Instead, it read:

G.L. Wood, Scientific Illustrator

It couldn't be. It was like she was seeing back through time to the woman her mother had been before daddy lost his job, started riding the bottle. For some reason, she'd thought that once Mama left, she would come to find her and Max would be responsible for helping fix her, getting her back together. Never had it occurred to her that her mother would have her own plan. One that didn't include her daughter.

Fury rose behind her eyes, glazing the screen with a reddish haze. Max stabbed at the play button, but upon hearing the woman's voice wield a tender confidence, it drew her in despite her anger. And why was she so angry? Her mother was a victim as well. She hadn't been that angry with the woman at the bank, who she could tell had taken verbal whippings of her own. Why did Mama have to be different?

Realizing she hadn't heard anything her mother—excuse her, G.L. Wood—said, she backed up the video to the beginning of her introduction. There, Dr. Novye smiling, saying her name like it was a dessert he had long denied himself that he was finally ordering. The soft "no," followed by the softer "okay." Then her mother's image. Max blew it up to full screen.

Her hair was different, cut to a fluffy TWA, that made her look like a boss. Gold studs in her ears reflected light onto her glowing brown cheeks. She laughed, flashing a tiny gap between her front teeth. Then the video stopped.

"What the fuck?"

It was only the first minute of a longer video and she'd been dropped from it. Did it require signing up to see the rest? It did.

"Damn."

She didn't want to, but she needed to see the rest of the video. She needed to hear her mother's voice. Hear what she had to say. If she were being honest, she wanted to ask her own questions. Why didn't you empty the safe deposit box? What are those cubes? Why didn't you come and find me and tell me you were okay? I worried.

Sometimes.

Sometimes she'd worried. Other times she'd gone for days, weeks without thinking about her mother. She'd spent so much time getting herself figured out that she hadn't called to check on Mama often enough. Then when she did call, their talk was rarely long. Either Mama was talking about the same things that she'd heard countless times: what she was making for dinner, what her old boyfriend was doing now, people she didn't know who had died, that Maxine tuned her out, only answering with grunts and sounds of acknowledgement so her mother didn't think the line had gone dead. Never anything about how she was going to leave Daddy. Max had gotten so furious and frustrated at her inaction, that without realizing it, her voice raised and she was a heartbeat from shouting at her mother to just do something!

The last time they spoke, Max had yelled. Had asked why she didn't come to D.C. and live with her. They'd call the police if Daddy came after them.

"Please don't yell at me like that, Maxine. I am not going to send another Black man to jail, so stop asking me to."

Her calm reply had stopped Max's tirade. "You have a knack for making me sound stupid, don't you? I'm worried, I'm scared for you. Why can't you see that?"

"I see that, but I have to do this my way."

"Whatever. I'll be involved when I come see you in the hospital."

"I have to go, baby. You take care of yourself." She quietly put down the phone, leaving the dial tone to buzz in her daughter's ear.

That memory of her callousness to a woman who had saved her, who was still suffering herself, flayed her open like one of her mother's entomological drawings. The feedback form was grayed out and her other searches for "G.L. Wood" online turned out nothing except this university laboratory website that she was currently on. She took out her wallet and signed up for membership to the site.

After confirming she was not a robot, the site gave her access. First thing was to play the entire video, skipping ahead to the part where mama appeared. For long moments, she looped the video, listening to her mother sound … was that happy? Did she even think of her daughter? From the smooth brow she had for a sixty-seven year old woman, it was clear she didn't think about Daddy. Her voice was warm and her smile was no longer the fake *everything is fine, don't say anything, don't mess up* one she'd gotten so used to. If this was the way her mother was before Daddy, she really wanted to know this woman.

The next video in the series began playing, and while the doctor spoke, it was her mother's hands pointing out specific sections on her own drawings of the moths and butterflies.

"Don't forget, they would eat you if they could," Dr. Novye said with his intense smile. "Your sweat, your tears, even your urine, it's all irresistible to these beautiful creatures."

Her mother held up the drawing and the camera zoomed in on the insect's face, right above Mama's manicured nail. "This vampire moth is from the genus *Calyptra*. They have a proboscis or haustellum that can get through even an elephant's skin."

Dr. Novye looked pleased, giving Mama his rictus smile before turning to the front again. "Exactly right. We've studied these creatures extensively and we have found and identified over fourteen species. So exciting to find out what these creatures can tell us about themselves and how they can further humanity's existence."

Letting the video run, Max opened up the contact page, addressing her message to G.L. Wood.

Dear Ms. Wood.
I'm your daughter.

Backspace.

Dear Ms. Wood,
I don't know if you remember

Backspace backspace

There was no telling who would be reading this email or if it would ever reach Ms. Wood. But suppose Max was wrong. Suppose this was not her mother? She'd just end up looking like some kind of crazy, messed up fool with mama issues.

So what? Ain't nothing wrong with being crazy.

Max laughed, hit the heel of her hand against her head, two, three times. Sometimes she had to laugh to keep from crying. Life had taught her that. She returned to the message box and its blinking cursor.

Dear Ms. Wood,

My name is Maxine Forest. I've recently returned to Charleston and I believe I've found some of your earlier drawings of various insects. They're in a safe place. If you'd like them returned to you or want to see them, please email me.

Look forward to hearing from you,
Max

She typed in her email address even though the contact form had asked for it as well. It didn't hurt to be extra sure. It was a feeling she hadn't had in a while. Mentally exhausted from that non-interaction, she closed the laptop and headed for the sofa.

ELEVEN

Her phone buzzed.

Again.

Again.

Maxine groaned, turned toward the sound. How in the world had she fallen asleep again?

Bleary-eyed, she grasped for the phone. Flipped it into life, squinting at the brightest light she could ever recall seeing. An email from the institute:

From: G.L. Wood (glwood@entomologyinst.org)

To: SeenMaxine@ourwurrld.com

Date: 2:14 a.m. Feb 20

Maxie, that you?

She bit her lip. Three words from the mother she hadn't lain eyes on in seven years. She pulled back her arm to throw the phone. No. This was her only lifeline to the world. She couldn't afford to break it. Break anything. She lay back on the couch, pulled her legs to her, turned into the stretch of pain in her leg to clear her head. This wasn't how she expected their reunion to go. It was almost as if her mother had thought she was gone from her life and was shocked to hear about her, much less from her.

She replied and they began an email exchange Max thought would have been better over text.

Yes, It's me. Can we talk? Can I call you?

It's long distance.

Chicago isn't that far.

No, I'm on mobile, not in my office. How about a video call? I can send you a link.

She noticed her mother using the European term for a cell phone, like Dr. Novye would probably do. Pushing that info aside, she agreed.

Okay. That's fine.

After scuttling off to the bathroom to check her eyes and teeth were clean, she splashed water on her face. It looked ashy and dry. It also looked lined, grainy, like an old photograph. She rubbed her face with a towel, put on some lotion she found on the sink, then sneezed, her entire head feeling like a bouquet, like she was drinking perfume, and she gagged.

She scrubbed her hands and face again but the scent lingered. After sorting through the laundry she'd done on her arrival, she found a t-shirt and shook out most of the wrinkles. Mama was such a stickler for clean and neat, she'd probably have so much to say about how Max looked but there was no time to do better.

Seven minutes later, the link had arrived. Max was ready. Or thought she was. Her heart didn't know what to do and alternated between racing at top speed and shuddering to a stop every few moments. She sat on the sofa with the low back, settling into the worn cushions. The link pulsated when she clicked it, the text turning from black to blue to purple, those bruise colors she was so familiar with.

Connecting…

To her surprise, Mama didn't comment on her weight or her hair or her lack of makeup. She just smiled a smile that Max couldn't recall seeing for a long, long time. And said,

"You look good, baby."

"Thanks… Ma," she whispered back.

"How are you? I mean really."

"I got the letter about the safe box. That's how I knew you left Daddy."

A pause during which G.L. Wood ran her hands over her hair. Max noticed the place where her ring used to be wasn't paler than the rest of hands. So it had been a little while, then. "I should have told you what my plans were but I had to make sure everything went right. I couldn't risk—"

"It's okay." What else could she say? It had been so long. Since they'd talked about anything other than safe matters that lay on the surface of their real emotions like a layer of oil over water. "Are you okay?"

"I'm good. Real good." Her radiance came through the screen and for a second Max envied her that joy, that happiness. Then that perverse imp faded away like so much mist under the sunlight of her mother's smile.

"I'm glad." Max stretched out her leg, propping it up on one of the chairs in the room. "I came and cleared out the box. Your drawings were in there and some other strange stuff. I don't know if you want it, but I can send it. Daddy's not here, so I—"

Mama's face fell, her jaw slackening and showing a bit of her age. "What? What do you mean—where are you?" She moved left and right, trying to look over Max's shoulder, but the camera on her phone wasn't a wide angle lens.

"I'm home. At the house. It's okay, I said Daddy's not here. Not the entire two days I've been here."

"Oh my god."

Mama's camera angle was wider. It showed what looked like a well-appointed hotel room, or maybe it was B&B or something. Lots of pinewood and open space, light-colored fabrics. She stood up, closed a door, returned to the camera, eyes wide with fear.

"Don't stay at the house. Your father—"

"Relax, Ma. I said he'd not here."

Her eyes were plates when she said, "Yes, he is, baby."

Baby. That word, drawing her back through time again, to a moment when she had to listen. When Mama would tell her warning stories, cautionary tales on how to avoid danger. What Daddy's mouth looked like when he was about to get angry, the shift in someone's voice when they were about to hurt you, the deep breath of someone about to savor your pain and hurt. When to run. To get away.

"What… how? I can't…"

"Do you know how caterpillars become butterflies?"

The sudden shift in conversation stopped her rogue train of thought and she answered without thinking at all. "Yeah, I went to first grade."

Mama ignored her snarky comment. "Maxie."

"Fine." She leaned back into the cushions, wondering what Daddy had done to make Mama lose herself like this. "They eat a lot, then spin cocoons. Inside there, they dissolve, and come out as different creatures."

A long sigh and Mama buried her face in her hands. "Almost, Maxie."

G.L. Wood lowered her hands and looked at the screen. She was her mother, only in business mode, her voice crisp, the warmth in it strictly professional. "Moth larvae make cocoons. Butterfly larvae make a chrysalis."

"So? What's the difference?" She sat up, agitated now. Beginning to get angry with her mother. "And what does this have to do with Daddy still being here? He's not in the house. I looked in every room."

"Moth larvae spin cocoons made of their own silk, similar to what spiders use to spin webs. A chrysalis... well, it's the caterpillar's own body. Effectively its skin expands, then hardens into what we call a chrysalis."

Max blinked, trying to understand. "Okaaay..."

"Then as you said, its body breaks down. Or almost." The woman stared into the distance, a frown between her brows.

"Mama!"

"Yes. Right. The caterpillar dissolves completely except for what are called imaginal cells. Like imagination. They're sort of stem cells which use the dissolved goo to make the body parts of the butterfly, legs, antennae, wings, all of it.

"Craig, I mean, Dr. Novye was able to isolate these cells and was thinking of ways they could be used to help people who have lost body parts or needed skin grafts, whatever. He knew I wanted to leave your father and that he would never let me go. So I asked him to send me some samples."

Max was traveling again, falling through time at top speed, her mind trying, trying to understand the words directed at her.

"It was the only way I could get out. I tried once when he was on one of his drinking benders, but he found me. I thought... I thought if he was compelled... biologically to make a chrysalis, I'd have time. Space to leave. It was just putting those sugar cubes in his drinks.

Even in the decanter of whiskey. I don't know who else he had over there drinking…"

"Oh, my god." The dark spots on the walls, behind the curtains. No food in the house. How many times had he made… how often had he changed?

The calm professionalism of G.L. Wood was gone now. Mama blubbered at her on the call. "I never thought you would go back to that house." She was typing, searching the screen. "I can't get there. We're in Finland now, at a conference. There aren't any more flights until—"

Typing stopped. Both rooms the women were in resounded with sudden stillness, a joint recognition of what was occurring around Max. The processes that were likely occurring.

"Neither one of us knows how long the process will take. Or how many times he'd been through the process already. Or what he'll be now. Maxie… you have to leave."

Mama's voice sounded far away. Miles. Years away.

He'd been here all along. Daddy was home.

TWELVE

She looked at her mother's earnest face and wondered when she had lost her mind. Maxine's body flushed with heat, embarrassed to see what her mother had become. So lucid sounding, her gaze intent and filled with concern and fear. She reacted in the way she did when customers at the delivery company had shouted, hurled insults, threatened. Extricated herself as quickly as possible.

"I have to go, Mama."

"But Maxie, you need to—"

"I'll be fine. I remember."

She ended the call, the terrified look on her mother's face barely registering. How had she gone so wrong? It was her own fault, wasn't it? Max's? She'd known what Daddy was like and she should never have left Mama here with him alone. It had destroyed her, altered her perception of the world. Still, she was grateful that Dr. Novye had let her keep her job. Mama needed to be independent, but what she'd said was impossible.

But wasn't that what science, technology did? Make the imposs-ible…possible?

After pocketing her phone, Max headed through the house again. How could anyone be here? She'd been though every room.

There was no attic, no basement. Nowhere for anyone to hide. And even if there were someplace, why wait so long to reveal yourself? It didn't make sense. It had to be in Mama's mind, her last attempt at trying to protect her only child. When Max felt more together, she'd ask to see her, check on her and make sure she was all right.

First, she had to check on the house. Just to be sure.

As she walked down the hallway, she berated herself for even considering the possibility that her mother's boss sent her an untested experiment to administer to her husband in order for her to successfully leave him.

Then she remembered the look he'd given her on the institute's video. How he'd asked her to be on camera and his gaze of pride when she finally agreed. That man gave a shit about her mother. She threw open the door to her bedroom, checked under the bed, the closet…

Nothing. Exactly as it had been when she got here. That was what…three days ago? Two? It was so hard to remember yesterday, but she could remember ten, twenty years ago. Easily. So easy, how it came back without her trying. Without warning.

The only room she hadn't searched completely was her parents' room. And the thought of doing it now made her skin itch. But she would do it…to be able to tell Mama that she was wrong. To reassure herself that her own father wasn't a beautiful monster.

Their room smelled, even stronger than before, if that was possible. It had a different stench this time, more like old blood than unwashed body. Metallic, sharp, rotted, the smell grew as she tiptoed further inside. The curtains were closed, and the mold stains in here were more plentiful than she'd seen in any other part of the house. Every corner had some darkened spot. Why hadn't she noticed this earlier? One of the spots was sunken in, as though whatever had taken hold of this part of the wall partially dissolved it to leave an indentation for itself. It was man-sized, and amorphously shaped, nestled in the corner furtherst from the window. What had happened in here?

Piles of dirty, smelly clothing on the floor, the chair…that was usual. Mama had done laundry while she lived here and Daddy never really got around to it anymore. She made her way through and around the piles toward the bed, careful not to lose her footing. It was unmade, sheets tangled, parts shredded as though someone had tried frantically to get out of them. The formerly white sheets were crusted with dried matter. Blood, feces, she couldn't tell and didn't want to. Wishing she had gloves, she grasped the cleanest-looking part of the sheet and yanked it from the bed. It came away with a sickening tear, the sound of a bandage leaving raw skin. Max dropped the sheet and it sank heavily to the floor.

Empty.

What had she expected? A skeleton? A corpse? She was greeted with another stain, human body shaped, but no body to be seen. Biting back her fear, Maxine eased one of her legs back, sinking to the floor. The other leg she curled under her to give her more balance. She wanted a pain pill, but they were addictive and the last thing she wanted was to become dependant. But it might have dull this fearful ache her heart was meting out.

It can't be true. Mama probably just killed him. How horrible the idea of that gave her comfort. Anything else, including finding him alive and well, was not a desired outcome. She leaned down, rolled on her side, holding her breath against the funk of the dirty clothes surrounding her. Looked under the bed.

Nothing there either.

Except for clumps of dust, the crowbar Daddy used for protection, and the odd slipper.

She was beginning to breathe easier. To compose in her head the email she would send Mama later, explaining that nothing had happened here and that Max would come see her and help her get herself together again. With a groan, she pushed herself backwards, dragging the crowbar with her, then rolled to a sitting position. She grasped the bedpost to help her stand, cursing her stiffness. If it was only longer, the crowbar, she could use it like a cane and help push herself up, lean her weight on it.

Instead, she carried it with her. If Daddy wasn't coming back, then he didn't need protection, she did. The crowbar would go under her bed. If Daddy or anyone else had a problem with that, they could get over it. Maxine hobbled to the closet and swung the door open.

She gasped, staggering back.

On the railing inside the closet, instead of clothing, there hung Daddy. Or not Daddy—a bloated imitation of his face and body, stretched to capacity. The chrysalis.

Maxine shuffled backward, not looking out for her footing and she toppled backward. She tried to twist her body to land gently, but her leg would not cooperate and she fell on her back, heavily, knocking the wind out of her and the crowbar left her grasp, thunking to floor. She stared up, exactly as she had done while she lay on the dirty floor of the bodega. Oh, she wanted to scream at the sight, but she had no breath in her lungs to get a sound out.

It clung to the ceiling by a multitude of legs, bent outward, then in. Wings the color of healing bruises caressed the ceiling, batting softly. A swirling mess of a pattern on those wings, as if it couldn't decide what it was going to be. Max saw what looked like a dark nipple on one wing, parts of fingers hung from another, like a grotesque imitation of a swallowtail. One complex eye rolled within a chamber too big for it. The squat body was segmented, and at the sight of Maxine, the head and abdomen bobbed up and down with excitement. Then the head bent down again, toward its chest.

Not chest, she corrected herself recalling her mother's labels on the drawings she did for the doctor. Thorax.

Sweet merciful Lord.

How long had it been there? Waiting? Why did she never think to look at the ceilings when she got home?

Max wriggled like a worm, trying to move, to get her breath back. Her fingers twitched, searching for the crowbar. The creature Mama created seemed to watch her, although Max couldn't be sure. Then, she knew it watched.

Slowly, it fluttered down like a falling leaf to land on the piles of clothes. It lifted two, three legs at a time as it marched toward her. She could only grunt, guttural sounds, as she tried to get her arms under her to scoot backward. Away. She wished she hadn't worn a dress, but they were easy to put on with her leg. They were also easy to hitch up and get wrapped around her legs, imprisoning her.

It came closer, braver now that she couldn't move well. One of its legs touched hers, and it fluttered its wings madly this time, enjoying her taste. That leg grasped hers, clawed feet digging in, as it continued to climb her prone form. She whimpered while she lay on the floor, begging it to go away. Telling herself it wasn't real. Her fingers waggled, searching for a way out.

Hiding under the bed was impossible. It was on her and she was only now getting her breath back. Her gasps were clumsy, stilted but she filled her lungs.

"Daddy!" she screamed.

It stopped a moment, head tilted as though it heard something. Its jaw—mandible, really—worked, sawing back and forth. Was it trying to answer?

"Daddy?"

The mouth opened, exposing a long, serrated proboscis. It poked at her leg, trying to get through the flesh. But the thickened, shiny keloid did not surrender easy. The scarred tissue resisted, and in frustration the creature reared up, fluttering madly.

Max managed to grasp the crowbar, bringing it across the side of its head. It connected with a crunch. While it was thrown back, it was undeterred. It had found a food source and it was not going to leave it. She hit at it again, but missed, her balance thrown off. It mounted her, sawing that serrated appendage into her skin. She shrieked, stabbing it in the thorax as much as she could. Its outer shell was so resistant, it was like it had fused with the hard shell of its chrysalis before emerging.

It found a softer bit of skin at her side, and opened it, as Maxine wailed, flailing. It slipped its hollow tongue into the opening and drank deeply. Frantically, she gripped the crowbar tighter, gasping as her strength faltered. Of everything her mother had told her of butterflies that belied their beauty, Max had never thought to remember this.

Did you know milkweed butterflies cannibalize their own caterpillars? I know, it sounds horrible, but they do. Rip them open and suck out their liquid.

"Daddy, don't do this." Its weight crushed her chest, making each breath a chore. Was that what it was doing? She stabbed it with the crowbar and it paid her little attention, moving its body around out of her way. It extended its wings as it drank, batting them in ecstasy.

Two hearts.

That feed the wings.

Max promised to give her mother and her doctor a piece of her mind once this was over. If she survived, that was. She turned the crowbar to the curved, bisected end and brought it down right between those waggling, finger-laced wings. It reared up, but Max held on, hooking it and pinning it to the floor with her own body weight. For long moments, she just held it there as it bucked, silent in its death throes. Then she used the crowbar to pull herself up to a sitting position to stab it again and again and again, until her arms burned with the effort and her leg throbbed with agony. She got to her feet again, with the help of the bed post and beat its hard exoskeleton until it cracked like crab legs.

At her feet, what had once been Daddy shuddered and fell still. Max heaved in a deep breath, then another, another until filling and emptying her lungs became a natural part of her again. Max moaned at the pain rocketing through her, as she dragged herself away from the gruesome scene to the kitchen. In the dryer she found a clean white t-shirt and covered the wound in her side, tying it off with a pair of her leggings. Tears leaked from her eyes, as she fought not to succumb to the horror of what she had done. The horror of what Mama had done. Which was worse?

Max went to the back door and swung it open wide, dragged out the remnants of her father, now unrecognizable as anything human and covered them with a tarp. Food for plants, blood and bone meal. Chum for insects and worms and the food crops she would plant over the enriched soil. They would eat you if they could. Once she'd sworn she'd never eat them, but history didn't always repeat. Things could change. Her outlook had changed, based on extreme circumstances.

Presumption of death. Section 62-5-07, rule five. How easily she'd memorized it.

A person whose death is not established under the preceding paragraphs who is absent for a continuous period of five years, during which he has not been heard from, and whose absence is not satisfactorily explained after diligent search or inquiry, is presumed to be dead.

She repeated it to herself like a litany. Once it got dark, she'd tug the heavy laden tarp to the garden, and turn it into the soil. Cover it back up with the dried hay and brambles and loose branches.

So much to do, Maxine thought, her mind grasping at list items in order to cling to sanity: gardening, laundry, groceries. The house was in need of a good, deep clean. But that could wait until she had a pain pill. Tomorrow she'd report Daddy missing, and start the clock. Five years. Not such a long time to wait. Not for what was rightly hers.

Afterword

The algorithm knows Maxine better than she knows herself. Here is the scientist, Dr. Novye, for whom her mother worked, with his bug eyes and strange posture. Then, a butterfly lands on her crab dip and helps itself. Max doesn't know it, but the universe is trying to warn her.

They would eat us, if they could.

And of course, they do. From blow flies to dermestid beetles, many insects feast upon us once we're corpses. But what if they could eat us while we're still alive? What if insects could grow to a size that would allow them to hold us down while they drank our blood and devoured our flesh?

Poor Max finds out exactly what that would be like.

Eden Royce masterfully layers these science fictional horrors with domestic drama. Max's father, with his alcoholism and accusations, his anger and resentment, creating a constant miasma of inescapable fear. Max's mother, simultaneously neglecting her child and teaching her how to placate a monster, trying to keep her daughter safe while also planning her own eventual escape.

And then there's the house. *Hollow Tongue* appears to be a haunted house story, at first glance, with the adult child's desperate and unwanted return to the site of their childhood Hell, a place where strange things have happened and are still happening. Of course, things have only gotten more strange since the heir fled. Without the need to pretend that everything is normal for a child's benefit, the situation has deteriorated. There's a film over the windows, a constant sense of being watched, and inexplicable holes in Max's underwear.

Like every good horror story protagonist, Max can't run again. She is, at last, trapped in this place, and forced to finally deal with the trauma of her youth. She must face the specter that haunts her: her father.

But her father has become something inhuman. Royce's description of the remains of his human body clinging to his insectoid form are harrowing, the kind of vision that drives a person mad. And rather than merely feeding on her fear, Max's father wants to feed upon her physical body. In a parody of familial relationships, the child he was once responsible for feeding becomes the very thing that will provide him sustenance. Literally.

We have to wonder: how much of Max's father still remains inside his new exoskeleton? He hesitates when she calls out to him, but the hunger is too great. He can't lose this chance to eat, can he? Or is he aware that he's attempting to devour his own child, and doesn't care?

Either seems equally possible.

Max is no longer a frightened little girl apologizing for her "stink." She's now an adult. She's lived a life, and she's faced death before. She laid on the floor motionless, in agony, while police officers stepped over her, assuming she was a corpse. She's been abandoned, both by her mother and her boyfriend, when she needed them the most.

These horrors didn't destroy her, though. Max has looked Death in the face and refused to capitulate. She's come for her inheritance, for what she is owed by the man who gave her nightmares her entire life, and she won't leave without it. Her father is no match for her, even in his terrifying new form.

Eden Royce reminds us that we all have a choice. We can let our trauma define us, drag us down, and make us hesitate. Or we can face it head-on, hit it with a crowbar, bury it in the backyard, and claim what's rightfully ours.

I don't know about you, but I'm looking for my crowbar.

Sarah Hans
Author of *Asylum*

About the Author

Eden Royce is a Shirley Jackson Award finalist and her short stories have appeared in a variety of publications, including *FIYAH Literary Magazine of Black Speculative Fiction*, *The Year's Best Dark Fantasy & Horror*, *Strange Horizons*, *Nightmare Magazine*, and *PseudoPod*. She has written articles for *Writer's Digest*, *The Horn Book Magazine*, and *We Need Diverse Books*.

Her debut novel *Root Magic* is a Walter Dean Myers Award Honoree, an Andre Norton Nebula Award Finalist, an Ignyte Award winner, and a Mythopoeic Fantasy Award winner for outstanding children's literature.

Find her online at edenroyce.com.